Apple Pie and Arsenic

A Small Town Culinary Cozy Mystery

Maple Lane Cozy Mysteries
Book 1

C. A. Phipps

Dedication

To the women in my special writing group—you know who you are—without you the Maple Lane Mysteries might never have eventuated. Certainly not the Titles!

You all contributed in some way and I will be eternally grateful for that and your friendship.

Women are strong, and stronger together.

Love Cheryl x

Apple Pie and Arsenic

Would you kill for pie?

Finding the body of her friend was a shock and when she's accused of the death, not only does Maddie want answers, she must find a way to clear her name.

As the timer ticks down in the race to find the murderer before Maddie's put in jail, or the body count climbs, she enlists the help of her friends—one of the furry variety.

Then there's the sheriff. Her ex-flame is as confused as she is when the mystery heats up with another batch of clues, but does he believe she's innocent?

If only solving murder were as easy as apple pie!

If you loved Murder, She Wrote, you'll enjoy Maddie's style because she's not taking no for an answer either.

The Maple Lane Mysteries are light, cozy mysteries

featuring a quirky cat-loving bakery owner who discovers she's a talented amateur sleuth.

Other books in The Maple Lane Mysteries
Sugar and Sliced - The Maple Lane Prequel
Book 1 Apple Pie and Arsenic
Book 2 Bagels and Blackmail
Book 3 Cookies and Chaos
Book 4 Doughnuts and Disaster
Book 5 Eclairs and Extortion
Book 6 Fudge and Frenemies
Book 7 Gingerbread and Gunshots
Book 8 Honey Cake and Homicide - preorder now!

Remember to join the new release mailing list and pick up a free recipe book.

Chapter One

Maple Falls, Population: 10,915.

Madeline Flynn read the sign as it went by and smiled fondly. You couldn't get much farther from New York City in distance or size—which was a breath of fresh air. Literally.

Maddie open the passenger window of the cab to breath in the smell of home as they came over one of the last hills to view the full vista of the town. With the crystal-clear waters of the lake behind and the mountains to the left, Maple Falls epitomized the 'clean and green' tag they'd been given long ago.

As usual in this location, the radio began to crackle with static and the driver changed stations to their local one. Noah Jackson, the DJ, was playing her kind of music: rock and country with a sprinkling of pop. Maddie tapped her fingers on the top of the door as her long blonde hair swirled behind her, a rarity since it wasn't often let out of the thick braid she preferred for work.

She would have cut it years ago, but her Granddad, rest his soul, had insisted Maddie keep it long like her Gran's.

Every time she thought seriously about seeing a hairdresser, his voice came back clearly.

"It's so beautiful, Maddie. Why would you get rid of a gift like that?"

It was impossible to go against the kind and gentle man she adored, and even after he'd gone she hadn't the heart to do so.

Pushing her hand into the breeze as they swept past farms with paddocks of cows, sheep, and others with crops, she relished the sense of freedom the drive from the airport was giving her. She couldn't wait to get behind the wheel of her Jeep, currently stored in Gran's garage, and cruise with the top down along familiar country lanes.

'Honey' was more than a mode of transport. Her grandfather had bought her for Maddie when she was sixteen and was a major source of good times for her and her close friends over the years. In fact, Maddie missed Honey—so-called because she was a rich, dark golden color—as if she were another friend and hated having to leave her behind almost as much as Suzy and Angel. New York City was no place for a country girl to drive, even if she'd been able to find or afford somewhere to park.

When she sighed, Bernie Davis shot her a sympathetic grin. "Nearly home, love. It's a shame you couldn't come back more often. With not being so well over the winter, Gran's sorely missed you. "

Was there a touch of censure in his statement? She wouldn't be at all surprised. They'd chatted about all sorts of things that weren't too personal, apart from the initial "'Hi, how are you?'" Clearly, the time had come for him to ask what the rest of the town would want to know. As the only taxi driver in town and the odd-job man for most of the population, it was expected that he would have the latest gossip on anyone entering or leaving Maple Falls. Especially if the passenger was one of their own.

Maddie sighed again. It was probably best to get a plausible response out there and avoid the question being asked 10,914 times, even if it annoyed her to have everyone know her business. Like it or not, Maple Falls was probably never going to change regarding that.

"It *has* been too long. I've been working hard and saving for my own bakery. A vacation hasn't been possible."

Bernie grinned. "Well, you're here now. Gran's been telling us how well you're doing, even after changing jobs. A bakery of your own in New York? You'll be more famous around here than you already are when that gets out."

Maddie brushed that aside, still feeling awkward at receiving praise from an entire town; especially when they'd expected more from the business degree scholarship she'd been awarded.

When she'd left college, she believed aiming for success in that arena was what she should be doing. After all, her marks in business studies had been what got her the scholarship. But as soon as the degree cooled in her hand and she was working her very first job, Maddie knew it was a mistake—a big one. Madeline Flynn was not made for sitting behind a desk. No, she was a working-with-her-hands type of girl.

She should have known, and maybe deep down she had but hadn't wanted to admit it. At the time, accepting that scholarship meant she felt obligated to make it work and desperately made herself fit into that world. Every day was torture. Even the wonderful outcomes when she helped people achieve their dreams didn't make her feel the way she did when she was baking. But baking was a hobby, not something she could make a career of. Or so she'd thought.

Going from a well-paid job to starting at the ground level in a bakery would be a terrible waste. For two years she told herself that. Finally, when she was completely miserable with her life, and despite a steady boyfriend who thought she was insane to consider throwing away her career, she knew the time had come to stop working at something she felt no passion for and she had called Gran.

Naturally, her grandmother hadn't said a word about the waste of a degree, wasn't at all surprised by Maddie's change of heart, and certainly didn't care what people thought.

When the opportunity to change careers arose, it was through a chance meeting with a woman who came to Maddie seeking help with marketing for a future venture. A venture that Maddie was naturally interested in since it revolved around owning a bakery. This shared dream ensured they became good friends and when Camille told her bosses at the bakery where she worked, all about Maddie, they'd called her in for an interview.

The sights and smells of the famous French bakery were heavenly, and Maddie's heart beat with the passion she'd been keeping under wraps. This was the life she wanted. Whether it was due to Camille's good word or her own over-the-top delight, the owners offered her a job starting at the bottom. It was a huge leap of faith for a family business that didn't generally hire outsiders, and Maddie liked to believe she was deserving of that faith.

Her heart knew it was the right choice, and with Gran's blessing, she'd jumped at the chance and never regretted her decision. However, a residual embarrassment lingered at being seen as a failure around Maple Falls.

"What's been happening here, Bernie?" She changed the subject.

"The usual. People stepping on toes and then having a drink over their apologies."

"Nothing new, then?"

They laughed together at the notion that their town might change in any way. Situated twenty miles south of the bigger town of Destiny, Maple Falls was a lot older, had charm in bucket-loads and almost everything a person needed.

Bernie suddenly frowned. "There is one bit of unsavory news. The mayor has been under fire from an anonymous source. I know Denise is a friend of yours, so I thought you might like to know she's struggling a bit."

Maddie had been happy to let Bernie talk while she enjoyed the scenery, but now he had her full attention. Denise was a lovely, big-hearted person, so to hear she was being harassed was upsetting. "How do you mean?"

"It's stuff in the paper and flyers appearing all over town about how she isn't living up to election promises of bringing in more tourists or boosting the economy in other ways."

"Surely Maple Falls is doing great for a small town?"

His brow creased at her tone. "Hey, don't shoot the messenger. I'm doing fine and so are most people, but gossip can spread and we do have a few members of our community that don't exactly share the same spirit as the rest."

Bernie was being tactful, but they both knew whom he was referring to. Maddie would be keeping an eye out for them and as much she might hate confrontation she wouldn't stand by and let Denise be hurt. She sighed. Not even home yet and she was already enmeshed in a Maple Falls drama.

"Sorry. I'm just surprised, because Denise has already done so much good."

He nodded as they crested the last hill, and there, stretching out before them, was the town itself. Once more, a peaceful feeling settled over her.

To the left were the vineyards. Row upon neat row stretched out to the mountains, with the small lake sparkling at their base. To the right was farmland. Rich and fertile, the land around Maple Falls was a beautiful myriad of colors that never dimmed even in winter.

At the bottom of the hill and on the outskirts of Maple Falls, Bernie slowed considerably. It was something people did automatically, even before the 30-mph sign was in view, because the old town was spectacularly beautiful and worth an unhurried look.

Especially now, in her best season, anyone who had a heart was bewitched by Maple Falls. Spring was when the old girl shrugged off the darker shades of winter and burst out into the colors of the rainbow, when every garden in every street blossomed as if in competition.

Maddie almost laughed again. There was no denying that the residents could be very competitive, from gardens to the annual spring fair, where they could showcase everything from flowers to baking, crafts to furniture making. Summer heralded the music festivals and farmers' markets, while fall was full of family fun, harvest festivals, and corn mazes to delight the young and old. Finally, there was the winter carnival and the time when Christmas decorating took center stage. There was always a season and an unwritten opportunity to go one better. Of course, it was all done good-naturedly.

A canopy of big-leafed maple trees shaded the main street and many of the ones intersecting it. They were enormous specimens of the Oregon native, some even reaching close to their top height of sixty feet.

The founding fathers' properties still stood interspersed along the main street with the businesses, the sheriff's department, and the fire station. Out of the three brothers who had founded Maple Falls in 1880, one descendant, Mickey Findlay, occupied one, while the others had long ago been sold to the town. Of those, one was now the doctor's office and a small pharmacy; the other was home to the Mayor's office and the community center.

They were impressive buildings which had been studiously maintained through the years. The community center was a hive of activity, serving as a meeting place for the older generation, who Gran presided over like a queen bee.

Maddie hadn't lived here for several years, although she had come home for most of the holidays until she changed jobs. That was when the questions about her use of the scholarship veiled thinly with disapproval began. Although a few things had changed, trees had grown, families had come and gone, businesses opened or closed, Gran and her best friend Angel were what always drew her back.

When they reached the center of town, a wave of nostalgia hit her. Here was a place, despite being the town's hub, which had the quiet grace only a small town could convey. The well-worn sidewalks and roads were spotlessly clean, as were the front yards of the locals who were rightly proud to live here.

It wasn't quiet because there were people around, but after living and working in the hustle and bustle of New York for a few years, for Maddie this was a direct contrast. People acknowledged each other. They stopped to chat and really listened to what a person had to say.

It was a relief to know the place where she'd grown up was still the same, and that the woman who'd raised her would be waiting to welcome her with open arms. Gran was more like a mother than a grandmother. She had taken Maddie in without hesitation when Maddie's mother had left town for a faster-paced life. With no father on the scene, maybe her grandparents had felt they had little choice, but they'd never made Maddie feel anything but loved.

Coming home meant so many things, but at the heart of her emotions was what the two of them shared. Because they were so alike in their love of baking and friends, it had been a wrench for Maddie to leave. And even at twenty-eight, it still was.

Maple Falls was where her heart lay when it came to a place to live, but she had been on the cusp of something really great in New York. Having looked into buying a bakery with a friend, she was so close to having her dream come true, she could taste it. Pun intended. Then Gran's SOS had come, and there was no other choice for Maddie but to come home to Maple Falls, because her feelings about letting people down were no match for how much she would do for Gran.

As they drove down Maple Lane, the main street, people waved as they went about their business. Isaac Carter ran the local diner, and he was writing the day's specials on the board outside. Maude Oliver, president of the Maple Falls Country Club and secretary of the town board, stopped poking the vegetables on display at Janet Mitchell's grocery store, and Jed Clayton, a sweet old man, was walking through the park, whistling for his dog. The grapevine would already be well into overdrive to say she was back, but there was nothing to be done about that.

Then they were turning into Plum Place. Now, this really was home. Maddie had walked all over town more times than she could remember, but this was her street, and she knew every inch of it.

Everything looked the same except for one of the shops. From the front, it appeared neglected compared to the others. From this side, it was almost derelict, which would not go down well with the town board.

Then they were past it and pulling into her grandmother's driveway. Wisteria graced the porch, the purple flowers hanging like succulent bunches of grapes. The rocker—exactly how old it was made an often-repeated conversation piece, since it had been there for three generations at least—was moving gently in the breeze.

Gran appeared in the doorway as if she'd been watching for Maddie. Knowing Gran, she probably had been. A marvel at nearly seventy, she'd recently admitted she was getting too old to maintain the family home she'd inherited from her parents. After a major bout of bronchitis last winter, she'd decided to sell. That had been a shock, but as much as it tugged her heartstrings, Maddie was here to help her find a new home. It was the least she could do.

The wonderful family bakery where Maddie currently worked with Camille, was in the heart of Manhattan and did a flourishing trade. In fact, they were one of the busiest in the city, and they needed every pair of hands right now. They'd granted her a week for this unplanned break, and if that wasn't enough time to get the ball rolling, Maddie wasn't sure what would happen. The one thing she did know was Gran wouldn't choose the first place she saw. She was a thinker, and that generally took time.

It was difficult to think of Gran as old. Her ramrod-straight back and salt and pepper hair tucked neatly into a bun looked the same as they had for years, as did her smile

11

and floral apron. Both were her trademarks, and one rarely appeared without the other.

"Hello, darling," she called out as Maddie got out of the taxi. "Good timing. I've just pulled an apple pie from the oven."

Chapter Two

Maddie could smell the pie from where she was standing, and Bernie had a hopeful glint in his eyes. Once you'd tried Gran's baking, nothing ever tasted as good. People came from miles away, paying her to make birthday cakes and delicious baked treats, and had done so for years. More often than not, she took less money than she should, and it was agreed by all her customers that whatever treat she made and whatever she charged was certainly worth it.

Bernie opened the back of his van and carefully pulled out a large cage and set it on the grass beside the driveway. Once he'd taken her bag to the porch, Maddie gave him his fare and added a hefty tip for his trouble. Not everyone wanted a cat like hers in their vehicle, but Bernie never raised an eyebrow, and he always did the lifting, which was a marked difference from New York City cabbies.

"Just you wait a minute," Gran said to Bernie.

He grinned in anticipation. No-one went away from here without something to eat.

Then she gave Maddie a hug. They hugged hard, the way Maddie had been taught. The Flynn mantra was "hug someone like you mean it, or don't bother."

She savored the smell of apples and cinnamon, which was Gran's brand of perfume. One that couldn't be bought. One that meant love and home.

Gran smiled, a little misty-eyed, when they let go and went inside to fix a plate for Bernie.

Big Red yawned as Maddie opened his cage, then jumped out onto the grass as gracefully as he was able. "I'll be inside," she told him, giving his arched back the expected scratch.

The big Maine Coon gave her a disgruntled look, stretched, and with a flick of his tail sashayed over to the shade of the maple tree that dominated the front yard.

Poor boy. She could appreciate that his trip had been a great deal less comfortable than hers. Even with the air conditioning on, the taxi had been hot, and what the plane had been like for him, she hated to think. He wasn't a cage kind of animal, and he would only get into it with great reluctance and many treats.

For such a short visit, she would ordinarily leave Big Red in the kennels, but they'd let her know last time that Big Red wasn't welcome back—something to do with asserting his authority overzealously with his peers.

Despite Gran's ill health, a couple of incidents involving her ex-boyfriend who was involved in dodgy dealings made getting away from Manhattan more enticing. However, Maddie refused to give that any head space at all. It was wonderful to be home.

Gran came out with the covered plate and handed it to Bernie who looked as excited as a child at Christmas. "I'll expect that plate back next time you're passing," she said.

"Much appreciated and I will." He touched his cap and carried it carefully back to his car as if he held precious gems.

"Welcome home," Gran called out to Big Red. She gave a wry smile as Maddie joined her on the porch. "He looks cross. I guess he'll come in when he's ready."

"You know him so well." Maddie grinned. "Now, tell me how you really are. I've been so worried since your call. I'm sorry it's taken a couple of weeks to get here."

Gran waved her apron at the fuss. "I'm doing great, and I'd have been pleased to see you any time you could make it. I certainly didn't expect you to be on the next plane."

Maddie had thought Gran might resist her help when she'd called to say she was on her way home. When no resistance was forthcoming, she'd assumed the worst. "I'm so glad you're doing a lot better than I was anticipating."

"Goodness, did I give the impression I was on death's door?" Gran chuckled. "The bronchitis was bad, but the cough's nearly gone. Although, I do admit that the packing seems to have made me a little maudlin."

Maddie put an arm around her as they walked through to the kitchen, leaving her bag for later. "It's only natural. This is your home, and you've lived here all your life."

Gran squeezed her waist. "Like you."

They were the same height of 5'7" and had similar builds. When Maddie looked at pictures of her childhood and compared them to Gran's, they looked so alike that they could have been sisters. For a child without parents, that was a big deal.

"Yes, that's true, but I've also lived other places now. Not that I won't shed a tear or two when you sell, but I'm sure it won't be as painful for me as it will be for you."

"That you understand means a great deal to me, sweetheart. I sure hope you don't mind using your vacation time to help me out. I hate to be a bother."

"Psssh! You could never be a bother, so don't give it a thought. Where else would I take a vacation? Plus, I wouldn't have let you do this by yourself. Real estate agents can be hard to deal with, and you'll want to get a good price."

"I know you don't take nearly enough vacation time, but I'm grateful you're here now. The thought of tackling this on my own was pretty terrifying," Gran sniffed, pinching the bridge of her nose. "Your granddad took care of the big things. Tea?"

They might occasionally talk about being upset, but being staunch was also a major factor in their DNA. They were tough, and they liked it that way.

Gran's daughter, aka Maddie's mom, had been a handful, according to Gran. Ava Flynn broke both their hearts when she left, even though they'd tried every way they could think of to show her they loved her. It had gnawed at the young Maddie, and she knew it had affected Gran because she would sometimes catch her staring at a photo of Granddad and Mom.

Fifteen years later, Maddie's mother was still missed, but they had moved on from being sad, and tea was still the magic potion for everything. Being an Anglophile, anything English was close to Gran's heart, but tea was her main legacy from her parents. Born and raised in Bath, they had emigrated to America when Gran was a teenager, but she'd never forgotten her roots.

Her kitchen had shelves filled with an assortment of bric-a-brac that all in some way represented England. Single sets of matching cups and saucers with side plates, tea canisters with pictures of the royal family adorning them, and many teapots in a similar vein were lovingly dusted on a regular basis.

"I'd love a cup," Maddie said. "In fact, I need one. The traffic was horrible until we got past Portland. I hope one day they build an airport in Oregon closer to Maple Falls that's big enough to handle passenger planes." The one in Destiny was for light planes and helicopters, all privately owned.

Gran carefully took two cups and saucers from the shelf, along with side plates, while Maddie filled the kettle. It was an old relic passed down by Gran's mother, who had died long before Maddie was born and had instilled in her daughter the art of tea-making. Each set of cups and saucers was different and often had not been purchased together.

Over time, Gran had accumulated more than a dozen sets. If a person came for tea more than a couple of times, a particular set became theirs. Maddie always used the one with a pink rose, while Gran's favorite had lilacs.

"I haven't been to Portland since you were last home. Actually, it doesn't interest me to go far these days."

Maddie was plugging in the electric kettle that was as important as the best brand of tea that Gran insisted on using. She turned quickly. "You'd tell me if you were still unwell, wouldn't you?"

"Of course I would. Why do you ask?"

"You've always loved your weekly jaunts to anywhere the buses or trains would take you, and you've said more than once that you'd have to be taken out of this house in a coffin to get you to leave."

Gran laughed. "I did say that didn't I? But things change, and I have to be realistic. I'm no longer a spring chicken. I'm also thinking about handing over the leadership of the community group to some younger blood."

"What? No way. Those ladies depend on you to liven things up around here." The club had been founded by Gran and a couple of her best friends, and they were forever searching for places to go and speakers who loved interesting things.

"That's the thing," Gran said. "They need to change it up. This is the twenty-first century, for goodness' sake. There must be other things to do that I've never heard of."

Maddie snorted at the idea of that group of women "changing things up". They were the happiest bunch of older men and women, doing what they loved, but perhaps not all as open to change as Gran.

Still, the club had played a big part in Gran's life, especially after Maddie left. Since Gran had never learned to drive, a bus or taxi was the only way for her to get around unless someone offered her a ride to Destiny. Every month, she organized the community group jaunt to somewhere as a day trip, as well as their speakers. It was a shock for Maddie to hear her giving up on it. Who would take that task on now?

Gran liked to be busy, and she also walked for miles. At least, she always had. She looked so healthy and fit, Maddie had a hard time thinking of her as either old or sickly.

"It's been good for me to be the president for so long, and it was something to keep me busy while you were away, but I'm over it," Gran continued. "I've been everywhere several dozen times, and now I can honestly say that staying around home is far more appealing."

"Except you're moving."

"That's true, but a home is whom you fill it with, not wood and nails."

Maddie's eyes prickled with tears, and she felt a distinct twinge of regret at the idea of someone else living here. Still, this was Gran's decision, not hers. She sucked up her sadness and smiled as she warmed the teapot and added English Breakfast tea leaves, their favorite, then filled it with boiling water.

"It's so nice to be back in Maple Falls and out of the rat race, but I only have a week, which means we need to get on to finding you a new place, pronto."

They sat at the old oak table, which had been scrubbed so often that it was now much paler than it had started out. Gran pushed a pile of brochures and papers at Maddie, as well as a large slice of pie. It was still warm, and Maddie took a forkful, then closed her eyes.

"Mmmm. I've missed your baking."

"I'm sure that after all that training in a French patisserie, yours is just as good, if not better."

Maddie tilted her head, savoring the pie. "Not quite. But it's getting close."

Honesty had been a strong part of growing up with Gran, who couldn't abide lies, so there was no point in false modesty. But how could you compare your own food with that of the woman whose recipes were loved by so many, and from whom you had begun to learn your craft? Gran had founded and fueled Maddie's passion for baking, a passion that had never waned.

She took another bite of pie. Yep, this was heaven on a plate. Gran was sitting across from her, patiently waiting for a decent pause, or for her to finish, whichever came first. Reluctantly, she put down her fork and spread out the brochures. Selling the family home was the right thing to do, but that didn't make it easier. These walls held so many memories—most of them happy.

Her heart sank at the sight of so many places to view. "Do you want to see all of these?"

"I've circled a few that may be of interest, but I wanted to discuss another option."

Maddie knew that tone. Gran could be very persuasive in general, but when she adopted that tone, you could bet something you weren't ready for was about to hit you squarely in the face and would probably stick like strawberry jam.

She took a few sips of the strong brew then a deep breath. "Okay. I'm ready. Tell me what you're up to."

Gran grimaced. "You're being a little dramatic, and it's not like I'd force anything on you."

She completely ignored Maddie's open mouth at the unfamiliar censure and tapped the top brochure.

"Here's the retirement community Angel took me to visit. It's quite nice, but they have a 'no overnight guests' policy, meaning you couldn't stay with me. I don't like that idea one bit." She turned it over and replaced it with several more. "There are these."

She flicked each one by Maddie's nose. Very fast. Maddie waited for the bomb to drop, and fortunately she only had to suffer the blur of papers for another few seconds.

"Then there's this. Now, I know you have your own plans, but please don't say no right away. Read it, go see it, then decide. Okay?"

Gran had begun to look jittery as she waved the paper in front of Maddie.

"Good gravy. How bad can this be? My nerves are turning to custard."

The slightly wrinkled chin lifted defiantly. "It's not bad

at all. In fact, it's a wonderful opportunity if you can see the potential like I do."

Maddie pulled the paper from her hand so quickly that a small corner of it remained in Gran's fingertips. The front of the brochure was graced with a picture of a familiar block of four stores. A red rectangle was around one of them—the one Maddie noticed looked unkempt. At the end of the block, it not only sat on the main street of Maple Lane but backed onto Plum Place. Just up the road.

"I don't understand. You've decided to sell the house because it's too much. Why would you want a shop?"

Gran's eyebrows shot up. "For a bakery, of course. If I buy the shop, that one there"—she pointed at the red one—"it comes with a two-bedroom apartment upstairs, and since they all back onto our road, they have small yards of their own. It's a bit tired, but we've redecorated this house, so I know we can do the same to the shop and the apartment to make it just as lovely."

Maddie shut her gaping mouth with a snap. "You're not making sense. You can't manage a shop!"

Gran looked astounded, as if Maddie had stupidly missed the point. But what, exactly, *was* the point?

"No, I couldn't, but you could."

"Me?" Maddie was as confused as confectioners' sugar pretending to be frosting.

"For goodness' sake. I'm not speaking a foreign language. Isn't that your dream? To open your own bakery?"

Still feeling as if she were in an alternate universe, Maddie nodded. "Sure, but not here."

Gran sniffed. "Why not? I'd have thought Maple Lane was a perfect location."

Maddie had no idea what had brought on this weird

conversation, but she wasn't liking where it was going. "It would be if I didn't plan on opening a bakery in New York City someday soon."

"It would be much cheaper to open one here."

Maddie tried to keep the frustration out of her voice. "That's true, but I don't have the money yet to buy a shop outright."

"Don't get prickly. I appreciate all of that. First, the owner is desperate to sell, so it's going for a song. Second, what if I put money in? I have savings. Or I could buy the whole thing outright with the sale from this place, and you could pay me back when you can."

Maddie was stunned for a moment. "No, Gran, I'm not taking your money. You've done so much for me already."

"I've done what family does when they love each other, nothing more. Anyway, you know everything I have will come to you when I'm pushing up daisies."

Maddie knew Gran wanted her back home, but this talk of not being around was scary, and it made her think once more that Gran might be sick and not telling her.

"You're not putting all your money into something that has no guarantee of success. I'll come home if you need me, but I'm not buying a shop in Maple Falls."

Gran looked down for a moment. When she raised her head, she tried to smile but failed miserably. "I totally understand. You should follow your heart and do what's right for you. Let's not talk about it anymore today. We can discuss more options tomorrow. Maybe I should rethink the retirement community."

Minutes ago, Gran had been excited about the prospect of going into business together, and now she looked utterly despondent. Was Maddie the worst granddaughter ever?

She sure felt like it. Each bite turned to sawdust in her mouth.

This wasn't a good start. If Gran had her heart set on the business and the apartment, then one week would never be enough to talk her into something else. Clearly it couldn't be the retirement community if even the thought of it made her miserable.

A germ of an idea took hold, and Maddie grasped it with both hands. The shops had been there for decades, and the one Gran was talking about looked truly awful from the outside. The inside had to be as bad. Probably worse. Maybe if they took a look at it and Gran saw how much they'd have to do to get it up and running, she would change her mind.

Pleased with that idea and hopeful that they could find a nice place for Gran afterwards, she smiled. "On second thought, if you think it's worth our time, let's go see this place. After all, a look can't hurt, can it?"

Gran's face lit up once more. "Really? Now?"

Maddie raised an eyebrow. "Maybe I could finish my tea and pie?"

Gran leaned back with an air of satisfaction. "Take as long as you like. I'll give the agent a call in a minute. Should I say to meet her there in half an hour?"

Maddie spluttered her mouthful of tea over the pristine white tablecloth. She had the feeling that she'd just been played, but she couldn't think of anything to say in the face of such eagerness. She dabbed at the mess with a napkin while Gran brought the phone to the table.

She'd never made Maddie feel anything but wanted and loved, and doing anything to make Gran happy had never been an issue. Unfortunately, this felt like a step too far.

As soon as her plate was empty, Gran dialed the

number and it was then that Maddie realized whom she was calling. They both knew the owner of the local real estate business, and the thought of seeing Virginia Bolton, let alone discussing business with her, was enough to make Maddie's insides turn to jelly.

What a morning, and it wasn't done yet.

Chapter Three

When Maddie walked through the door of the disgusting mess that was Glitter and Gold, the old pawn shop, her thoughts of taking a quick look then having a conversation about how it couldn't work slipped bizarrely away. This was what she'd been dreaming of, although her dreams had a New York City setting.

The store itself was a perfect size. Despite the state of the place and the moth-eaten furniture as well as an awful smell of mold, she knew immediately where everything would go. That insight made her think of a recipe she might formulate. It would come together in her mind until she was able to visualize the finished product, without having baked it yet.

This place was bigger than the New York City space she'd been planning to buy, and the front shop area here was large enough so there would be space for tables and chairs. She could serve tea and coffee rather than just food to go.

"Obviously, it's pretty messed up, with holes in the

walls everywhere. It would be a mammoth job to make it good enough to house a bakery," Virginia sneered, as if the idea was ridiculous.

Gran moved between them. "Maddie's not frightened of hard work, are you, sweetheart?"

Maddie flexed her patience muscle. "It's bad, but not impossible."

Virginia shrugged. "I already have another interested party, so if you don't buy it, there's absolutely no problem."

Maddie couldn't get a handle on what was going on with Virginia. By all accounts, she had a steady business, possibly due to the fact that hers was the only agency in town, but surely sales weren't so good that she could afford to push people away. Did she want to sell the place, or was this one of those tactics she used to force a buyer's hand?

Whatever. Maddie wouldn't be rushed but something occurred to her. "Who else wants it?"

Virginia looked down her Roman nose. "I can't tell you that."

"I'm sure I can find out. Maple Falls can't keep secrets."

Virginia laughed, which was what Maddie had intended, but it was a singularly unpleasant sight. The woman's eyes went to slits, and her teeth clenched.

"You have no chance of that. Besides, what good would it do?"

Maddie wished she hadn't bothered trying to converse. "I have no idea."

Virginia watched her carefully as she spoke. "I don't suppose Gran told you that old man Willis's body was found right over there."

Maddie felt the blood rush from her face, and Gran, who had known Mr. Willis very well and taken him meals after his wife passed away, gasped loudly.

"When you say 'found', what do you mean?" Maddie asked.

Virginia shrugged. "He died. He was old, and he clearly couldn't look after himself."

Maddie took exception to the way Virginia looked at Gran when she made the statement. "Still, it must have been a shock for his family."

"You'd think so, but they were pretty quick to put the shop up for sale once he was buried."

Things like that happened, Maddie told herself; it was natural. But it made her feel a little ill at the idea of living and cooking in a place where someone had recently died. Not that there was so much as a stain on the threadbare carpet.

Gran retreated into the kitchenette, which, because of its lack of even a cursory cleaning, was the last place anyone would want to be, apart from the hideous orange bathroom. She gave Maddie a small, apologetic smile. If someone had turned on a light bulb—not that it was an option since they were all missing—it couldn't have been clearer. The shop was just down the road from her house, and even if it hadn't been, everyone knew about the comings and goings of Maple Falls. Therefore, Gran had known about Mr. Willis's demise before Virginia delighted in telling them.

Virginia was watching them again, perhaps expecting a full-scale war. She didn't have a clue about their relationship, and Maddie wouldn't spare the time to enlighten her.

"I've seen enough," Maddie said. "We'll let you know soon. Let's go, Gran. We have a lot to discuss."

She ignored Virginia's glare as they left.

Gran followed, meek as a lamb, and waited until they got back to the house before she said a word, as if by the time they got there, Maddie would have calmed down and made the right decision. Whatever that might be.

"I know Virginia isn't your favorite person, but the poor girl is dealing with a very sick mother right now."

Maddie hadn't known that. "That's rough, but she's always been mean. Especially to me."

"Be that as it may. You could give her a little leeway. Why not pretend she isn't a factor in your decision, then see what you come up with?"

The fact that Virginia wasn't her favorite person had Maddie scrambling backward (like Big Red did when it came time for his shots) at the idea of doing any sort of deal with her, just as Gran had intimated. However, it could also be said that the woman didn't seem particularly inclined to sell her the place, either. She'd put out all kinds of negative vibes and brought up the death of Mr. Willis, encouraging Maddie to look elsewhere. That was odd behavior for someone whose life had always seemed centered around money.

Maddie sat at the kitchen table. "Please sit down, Gran."

Sheepishly, Gran did so. "I should have told you about Clive Willis. But I knew you'd be squeamish, and really, you shouldn't be."

"A person can't help how they feel."

"But they can. Here's the thing, sweetheart: people die all the time, and if we let it get the better of us... Well, half the population would probably be homeless if they chose not to live where someone had passed away. Maybe more."

Maddie was flabbergasted. "How did you reach that conclusion?"

"Logistics. If I died tomorrow and you moved back here, would you sell my house?" Gran asked patiently.

"No, but that's different."

"Is it?"

Maddie thought about it. "I can see your point."

Satisfied, Gran leaned back in her chair. "I knew you would."

"You still should have told me."

Gran frowned. "I'm sorry. Is it a definite no, then?"

Maddie pulled out her phone. "I need to talk to my friend in New York. We had plans to buy a place together. I hate to let her down."

"Oh. You never said it was a given." Gran sounded concerned, then she smiled. "Still, if she's your friend, she'll understand. I'll make tea."

Maddie shook her head at Gran's back. How Long had she been devising this plan? And now Gran could see no reason for it not to work out as she'd anticipated, no matter what was thrown her way.

Camille picked up at once, sounding delighted to hear from her. But from there, the call went as oddly as everything else that had happened today.

They spoke for some time, with Camille having a lot to say after Maddie explained what was happening in Maple Falls.

When they said their goodbyes, Maddie put her face in her hands, knowing what the outcome would be when she'd relayed all the news she'd just received.

After a while, Gran came over and put a cup of tea in front of her. "What did she say, sweetheart?"

Maddie rested her hands on the white tablecloth. "She said that when she told her family about our plans a couple of weeks ago, they were already negotiating with Camille's bosses to open another store that the family's going to run together. She didn't tell me before I left, in case you were really sick. She's delighted that I have a plan B and offered me a job any time if things don't work out here."

Gran patted her hand. "There you go. Things are falling into place, which means it's meant to be."

"But I only left New York last night. This is all surreal. Are you sure I'm not dreaming?"

"Sometimes we have to take the hand life deals us." Gran squeezed her arm.

Maddie took a sip of her tea, then rested her chin on her hand. "I guess."

"Why don't you sleep on it? We won't talk about it anymore today. You're probably still tired from your trip, and I've selfishly dragged you over to the shop and given you much more than you'd bargained for. You need to have dinner and an early night," she added.

Maddie nodded but didn't move. "Just to be clear. You really want this for us? Because it would need two people at least to make it work."

"I do, but only if it's something that could make you happy. If it isn't, then we'll look at other options. But, since I'll have plenty of time after giving up my time at the community center, it should work out fine. I'll fix us some dinner while you ponder things."

True to her word, Gran didn't mention the shop again, but she sang like a canary all evening until Maddie had to go to bed or go mad. She wanted her to be happy, but Gran was assuming an awful lot, and despite her eagerness, at her age would it be too much?

As she sank into the cozy bed in her old room, she began to relax. Coming home was a tonic. Usually. Big Red liked it too. Having finally forgiven her for the trip, he snuggled up beside her, his tail draped across her arm.

"What do you think? Should we move back home? It

would mean living over a shop, but you'd have your own yard, so it'd be a lot better than our place in Manhattan. Plus, no litter box."

He stretched, yawned in her face, and curled up ready for sleep, as if he didn't care one way or the other.

So, the question remained: a shop in Maple Falls—or a job in New York City?

Chapter Four

Tossing and turning, Maddie weighed the pros and cons of buying a mess of a shop in this small town instead of getting her much-needed sleep. It would have been far easier to get up and make a list, but she didn't want to wake Gran.

Throttle her, yes, for scaring Maddie about how sick she was and for withholding important facts like Virginia's involvement and Mr. Willis's death, which had made the shop available. Gran wasn't so sick or old that she wasn't able to bake, pack, and more importantly, decide on a business venture.

Regardless of how they'd gotten to this point, there were other things to consider. What would customers in Maple Falls want from a bakery?

Maddie doubted she'd be making too many fancy things for the clientele she could expect. That wasn't a bad thing, since that kind of baking was labor-intensive, and it would be just her and Gran to begin with.

Residents dining out were limited to O'Malley's Bar,

Isaac's diner, or going north to Destiny. If there were another option, one that excited them, they might be inclined to try it. Especially with Gran's baking on offer.

Maddie could offer celebration cakes for birthdays, anniversaries, graduations, and so on, which would definitely help her sales.

Finally, when sleep was clearly no longer on the agenda, she dressed and went downstairs with Big Red at her heels. Gran was already up, her eyes shining with interest, but she knew Maddie well and wouldn't force the issue until they were both on the same page. The trouble was that Maddie's page had been smeared into illegibility.

"Morning, Gran. I think I'll go for a walk before breakfast."

"Good idea, sweetheart. It'll clear your head, since it looks like you didn't get too much rest. I'll have pancakes ready when you get back. Blueberry ones."

Blueberry pancakes with maple syrup was Maddie's favorite breakfast. Gran wasn't averse to cooking coercion, and her cheerfulness was catching.

She had no destination in mind, but somehow her feet took her down Plum Place to the back of the shops with Big Red trotting beside her. Glitter and Gold was at the end of the block on a corner site, making the shop's back yard much larger than the others.

It too was a mess, but she could picture where she could grow herbs and other ingredients she'd need, to save on costs. It had been a long time since she'd spent any time in a garden, and her fingers were itching to get in there and make a start.

Big Red jumped up on the fence that enclosed the space and over to the other side, where he gave the yard a thorough inspection while she pondered how she'd gotten to this point.

She couldn't deny the feeling that she was being forced into this, even though she knew that if she told Gran she didn't want to do it, things would work out and their relationship would still be strong. Everything was falling into place, just like it had when she decided to go to New York City. Maybe Gran was right and this was meant to be. Dead body or no.

Maddie had always assumed she'd end up back in Maple Falls. The brash ways and the noise of a big city had been tough to get used to, but she was grateful for the opportunities she'd been given there. Now that Camille wasn't going to share in the costs of a business, buying something there was off the table; there was no chance Maddie could purchase a shop on her own. Which meant she would have to work for someone else for a very long time, or find another partner.

What better partner than a silent one, and one she knew? Plus, Gran could help out with the baking when necessary because Maddie wouldn't be able to afford to hire another baker. Perhaps she could hire an assistant and teach them the basics as a cheaper option.

As Gran had said, the price was great, and the seller wanted a quick closing. If they decided on a 50/50 partnership, and using their savings, Maddie would need to top off her share with a loan from the bank. This way, it wasn't as imperative that Gran's house be sold right away, which meant that they would have a place to live while they did the makeover.

Maddie's mind whirled as she followed the path around the corner to study the tired storefront. It was jarring compared to the others: the secondhand shop, which was one of Gran's favorite places, a butcher, and Angel's beauty parlor, whose neat storefronts were all in keeping with the rest of the town and its pride in keeping things neat and clean.

Maddie looked up to her best friend Angel's windows, but the bedroom was at the back, so it was hard to tell if she was awake. There was no reason to tell Angel she was back. The town grapevine would have done that for her, plus she'd phoned her friend before she'd left the city to tell her she was on her way.

In the middle of the intersection to her right, there was a small park with the biggest maple of all in the center. It was a wonderful place for picnics, with plenty of shade and a babbling brook nearby. She and her friends had spent a lot of time there, reading, studying and talking about boys.

She'd missed her 'Girlz', a name that Gran had coined for their tight group, and which many others had adopted. The three of them, Angel, Suzy, and Maddie, had been inseparable since they'd started school, and although Maddie had made friends in New York City, it wasn't the same.

Coming home would mean seeing them whenever she wanted, and more importantly, she would be with Gran, who wasn't getting any younger. There was an awful lot that appealed and much more that made sense.

With a jolt, Maddie realized it had taken a mere twenty-four hours for her to come to her decision. Suddenly, she couldn't wait to get back to the cottage, and she was almost running by the time she had rounded the block. Big Red thought it was a great game, and he pounced at her from fences and trees. Coming home seemed to be giving him a new lease on life, too.

The smell of pancakes made her stomach rumble as she walked up the path, and Gran was setting them down on the table when Maddie came into the kitchen.

Maddie threw her hands in the air in mock surrender. "You win. Let's buy the store."

Gran tried hard to keep the glee off her face, which made her look at least ten years younger. Her eyes twinkled, and she was all but giggling, an odd but wonderful sight. "You won't regret it. You'll be so successful, people will come from miles around to buy some of your baking. Mark my words."

Maddie folded her arms. "They'd better, otherwise we could lose everything."

"Don't be a gloomy Gladys. Positive thoughts and actions will get us where we need to go."

Maddie rolled her eyes, but Gran laughed again and hugged her even harder than usual. It was far easier to be optimistic when you had Gran in your corner, which was how Maddie had been brave enough to leave Maple Falls and this unconditional love in the first place.

After they sat down, Gran piled her plate and handed her the syrup.

"You can call Virginia after breakfast, if you like."

If she liked? No, she did not. She could almost hear the bell ring for round two with her nemesis.

She'd barely swallowed her first bite, which was amazing, when a perfunctory knock on the door was followed by a vision in rainbow hues.

"Morning! I hope you don't mind me busting in like this, but I had to see you before I open. Hey, Big Red, how's New York?"

Angeline Broome was a breath of fresh air. Even having lived in Oregon for years, she was still a southern belle.

Some might call her a ditzy blonde, but she was a force of nature, second only to Gran. After battling an awful childhood and an even worse marriage, she now owned her own beauty shop, something she had a real affinity for, and, since she was stunning, it was very appropriate.

Big Red, having heard her come up the path, greeted her at the door by twisting around her legs, and she almost fell a couple of times as she tried to get into the kitchen.

"Calm down, cat, and let the poor woman in." Maddie was just as happy to see her, but fearful for her wellbeing.

After hugs and kisses all round, Angel sat down. Gran immediately placed a cup of tea—the set with yellow daffodils—and a plate of pancakes in front of her, while Big Red sat between Maddie and Angel, waiting for a morsel to fall his way.

"I knew there'd be something wonderful on this table. I could smell it all the way over from my place as soon as I opened the window."

There was always food available for anyone who walked through the door, and it was assumed that anyone who entered would eat. Gran's English heritage was on fire when she had visitors, because to her, food was love.

That was fortunate for Angel, since she was always hungry. They ate in companionable silence with Gran looking on benevolently as they made short work of the pancakes.

Finally, Angel closed her eyes. "Oh my. These are your best yet."

"Hah. I thought so too," Maddie concurred.

Gran flicked imaginary dust from her apron. "Oh, you Girlz. They're the same as always. Do you want some more?"

"No, thank you," groaned Angel. "I really have to fly. I've got back-to-back clients, but I had to say welcome home. Let's catch up tonight if you can. Suzy and Laura are dying to see you."

Maddie didn't intend to look sorry over the inclusion of Laura, an attractive red-head, who for some reason seemed to dislike her, but she could feel reluctance written all over her face. Luckily, Gran and Angel assumed it was something else.

"Absolutely," Gran said. "You go out with your friends, sweetheart. We can't be packing every second."

Angel piped up, "Me and the Girlz would be only too happy to help out with that if you need us."

"It's not just the packing now, is it?" Maddie shared a look with Gran.

Angel was wiping her mouth on a napkin, but she saw the exchange. "Is everything okay here?"

"Everything is perfect," Gran said with an eyebrow raised at her granddaughter.

Maddie nodded at the shorthand. They trusted Angel, so they could tell her their news. "I'm not sure about perfect, but Gran and I are planning on buying Mr. Willis's shop. We're going to open a bakery if the family accepts our offer."

"Well, knock me down and call me blonde, I didn't see that coming. I thought the idea was to sell the house and move on."

"It was. But Gran had other ideas, which she'd kept to herself until yesterday. Ideas that included a meeting with Virginia."

Angel went bug-eyed. "We knew you'd be tired last night, and had things to discuss with Gran, so we let you be.

I wish I could have been at that meeting, though. Did she behave?"

"Let's just say she didn't spread out the welcome mat."

"I can imagine. She doesn't like me, but she really... doesn't like you."

Angel saw Gran's frown, and changed her tack. Maddie knew she'd been about to say that Virginia hated her, which was probably close to the mark, but Gran didn't like that kind of talk. She had her say, then moved on, and expected that was how everyone would behave when they encountered a person who didn't agree with them.

"Well, we're all different and we can't love everyone we meet. Isn't the shop a wonderful idea?" Gran asked Angel.

"It's fantastic, is what it is. My best friend is coming home to stay, and we'll own shops nearly side by side. What could be better?"

Maddie felt a rush of warmth for her best friend. With Angel wanting the world to love her, and Gran insisting they did, Maple Falls was a tonic for her skepticism.

"It hasn't happened yet, and I don't know when we'll find out about the sale. How about you all come by tonight anyway. You can lend a hand with some packing and we'll have a few drinks. Then we can either drown Gran's sorrows or celebrate when we do hear."

Angel stood and hugged them both. "My money's on celebrating. I'll call the Girlz, and we'll bring the wine."

They walked Angel to the porch, and when she'd gone, Maddie sighed. "Breakfast is done. I guess it's time to call Virginia."

Gran put her arm through Maddie's as they went inside. "Be nice."

"I'm always nice."

"Mostly, that's true."

Maddie laughed all the way to the kitchen, where the phone was, then took a moment to gather her thoughts. She was a customer, spending a lot of money. Virginia had better understand that.

If she didn't, Maddie would explain as "nicely" as possible.

Chapter Five

Bizarrely, after the first call, during which Virginia had reluctantly said she would present the offer to the family, Maddie's nemesis had been absent from her business and entrusted a minion to take care of the offer and the settlement. Maddie was glad about that, but if Gran was right and Virginia's mother was ill, she would have to find a way to be more tolerant. The daughter might be all kinds of mean, but Katherine Bolton was a sweetheart whom Gran adored.

Two days later the offer was accepted. Gran insisted they celebrate with the rest of the Girlz. That night with Gran's country music playing, fried chicken, potatoes, corn and salad ready and the table set, they sat on the porch waiting for their visitors. The setting sun shone through the trees dappling Plum Place and giving a fairylike glow to everything.

A small blue car turned into the road, and soon Suzy was coming up the path, followed by Angel. Behind them Laura walked slowly.

Maddie took a deep breath. Laura was Angel's friend and there was nothing to be done about her being here.

"Welcome," Gran beamed at them. "We're so glad you could come on short notice."

"We wouldn't miss it for the world. I'm so excited for you, and now we'll always be neighbors," squealed Angel as she hugged them both, referring to the fact that her salon was two doors down from the planned bakery.

Maddie's ears rebelled at the noise, but she hugged her right back. Suzy followed suit, handing over a bunch of flowers.

Laura hung back, looking around her. "You have a lovely place, Mrs. Flynn. I hope you don't mind me tagging along, but Angel insisted."

"Not at all, and thank you. I appreciate that no-one can refuse Angel." Gran smiled, took Laura's arm and pulled her inside. "Please sit everyone. Dinner is ready." She quickly added the extra place setting while Maddie pulled up another chair.

Fortunately, the Girlz kept up a barrage of questions which hid the fact that Maddie and Laura did not talk directly to each other. It was a mutual thing that had developed when Laura arrived in town a couple of years back and didn't seem to be getting better. Maddie couldn't pinpoint what the issue was, but Laura never seemed happy to see her or want to converse. It felt like she was hitting herself with a rolling pin each time, so she had simply stopped trying to engage with her.

"So, what's the plan of attack to get the business up and running?" Suzy asked. A pocket rocket—5'2" if she was lucky—with a mass of auburn curls that took forever to tame, she thrived on challenges.

"Perhaps you can come take a look when the sale goes

through and give me some advice, because it is in the worse state imaginable." Maddie grimaced.

"I bet it is. Poor Mr. Willis wouldn't have anyone in to help him when he started feeling sick. He sold what he could and shut the shop altogether."

Gran tutted. "I knew it was bad. I would bring him meals sometimes, but he was stubborn and insisted his son would take care of him. Initially, Ralph visited a couple of times a week, then it was more regular. That was when he began to keep everyone away saying his dad needed rest."

Suzy sighed. "Poor man, to die alone like that. His shop was not the nicest, but he seemed a genuine man."

"He was that, and rather sad. He never got over his wife leaving him. But enough of that, let's eat."

As they helped themselves to the food Angel topped up their glasses of wine.

"Let's concentrate on the celebration. Here's to Maple Falls's latest entrepreneurs! May your cookies never crumble."

They laughed and clinked glasses. Even Laura.

"If you need a hand with the cleaning up and decorating, we'll all pitch in, won't we?" Suzy looked around the table.

"Of course, as long as there's gloves." Angel wiggled her beautiful nails at them.

"Naturally. I'll get you yellow ones too." Maddie grinned.

"That would be much appreciated," added Gran.

Laura looked down at her empty plate and said nothing.

"What did your boss say?" Suzy asked.

"Handing in my notice was hard. I really liked the whole family. They were so kind to me and taught me everything I know apart from what Gran did, and I'll miss

Camille terribly. Hopefully, she'll be able to come visit one day." Maddie pushed through the sadness of leaving her friend behind to force a grin. "But look what I'll have instead. My own bakery. My dearest friends close by. My wonderful Gran by my side. That's plenty to be grateful for." She raised her glass. "To you. My family."

"Aww." Angel and Suzy responded, their glasses clinking on hers.

"I wish you all the luck, Maddie." Laura said quietly.

"Thanks." Maddie wasn't sure if Laura meant it or not, but she wasn't going to let it bother her tonight. Not when her dream was coming true.

Chapter Six

The next two weeks were spent organizing the loan with the bank and signing papers. Maddie used the time well, sourcing suppliers of everything from ovens and fridges to cash registers and fittings.

Back in New York City, Camille was kind enough to pack up Maddie's apartment, which she couldn't have afforded to carry on her own indefinitely. Finding a new roommate would have been daunting too. Those were both bonus things she wouldn't have to deal with now. Another was that Camille offered to buy the larger furniture, which would save Maddie a fortune in shipping. She'd also offered to send Maddie's personal things and smaller items by truck. Hopefully, they'd be here by the time she and Gran were ready to move into the apartment.

After they'd signed the final papers, Maddie allowed herself some elation mixed in with trepidation for the task she had in front of her. To have her dream come true was something special, and she vowed to herself that she would make it work because Gran losing any money from this venture was unthinkable, especially after all she had done for Maddie. Most of all, she was determined to show Gran how grateful she was for this opportunity.

Now, a month later, the store was coming together nicely. They'd taken the Girlz up on the offer to help decorate, and they were doing an awesome job. They'd spent every hour they could spare and were nearly as excited as Maddie—not only about the shop, but what this meant to them as a group. They'd often talked about her moving home at some point; she just hadn't expected it to become a reality this soon. Touched by their eagerness and how proud they were of her for making it happen, Maddie insisted that it had all been due to Gran. They said they didn't give a fig how or why, just that she was here.

Maybe she had to give up the idea of owning a New York City bakery, but having friends and family around was so much better. She'd been too busy while she was away to be aware of how much she missed everyone, and now being home made her so much happier. Besides, owning her own store anywhere had been the real dream.

As she painted the largest wall of the shop, she had a small misgiving. Laura had been included in the group since she became Angel's friend, but she hadn't set foot in the shop and seemed to be avoiding doing so. Something about being allergic to paint fumes.

"Hello?"

Maddie dropped the roller, sending a spray of paint over her coveralls, and turned to see a man bathed in sunlight in the doorway.

"Can I help you?" she asked as she put a hand up to shield her eyes.

"I guess you're not open yet, so cake is going to be out of the question."

He smiled as he came closer, and Maddie's heart made a quick flutter at the sound of the familiar voice, then several harder and more lengthy bangs at the sight of him. That tall figure with eyes so blue and a grin that lit up a room—there was no mistaking him.

"Hello, Ethan. I'm doing my best to get up and running by next week. I see you're still in the police department. Solving all the mysteries around town, are you?" she asked, as if seeing him up close was no big deal.

He removed his hat and touched his badge. "I'm the sheriff now, and there aren't too many mysteries around here. I see you're still a cook. Although I'm pretty sure that's paint on your cheek and not flour."

Looking at Ethan was like stepping back in time to when they were teenagers. Banter was the easy part but her cheeks got warmer. Foolishly, back then, they'd thought they were in love, and that things would stay the way they were forever.

"I'm a baker. There's a difference," she said, unable to think of anything else.

Ethan bowed a little. "Pardon me. A baker. Are you any good?"

He grinned, and her heart did that free-fall thing. He hadn't changed at all, which was annoying. He should have a pot belly or something that would make it easier not to remember what it felt like to be in his arms.

"You shouldn't tease a woman in charge of sharp knives."

"Tease? You know that's not my style," he said with feigned innocence.

"It's exactly your style. Some things apparently don't change."

He grinned again. "Like you. It's as if time has stood still from the day you left town."

She looked down at the curves that had replaced the skinny teenager and raised an eyebrow. "Not exactly. Plus, I'm sure I wasn't covered in paint."

"That just adds to the overall picture, and you look great. Better." He flushed a little, twisting the sheriff's hat in his hands. "I was at a seminar, then on vacation with my family, when you arrived back in town, and I've been busy playing catch-up at work. Otherwise, I would have come around sooner."

Maddie could see that coming here hadn't been as easy as he was trying to make out, which was rather touching. She didn't think she could have been the one to make the first approach, so it was a relief that he was here, despite the awkwardness they were both experiencing.

"I've been pretty busy myself."

"I'd say that's an understatement. You've moved home and bought a business in only a few weeks."

Maddie shrugged. "I guess it was meant to be. The family was in a hurry to sell, so the price was ridiculously low. And to be honest, buying this place wasn't my idea."

Ethan grinned. "The infamous Gran strikes again. She's the kind of woman most people want to listen to. She usually has great advice, and now she's finally found a way to bring you back to Maple Falls for good."

Maddie gave a wry smile. "You know what she's like. She'd made up her mind before I even knew our buying a shop together was possible."

He laughed, a sound she had always loved to hear. It had been Ethan she'd missed the most after she'd first left, even more than Gran, Angel, and Suzy. Their childhood crush had begun to die a natural death when he went away to college, and it was done by the time she told him she was moving to New York. It was funny how they'd both ended up back where they'd started.

Ethan came closer, looking like the awkward teenager she remembered. "When I heard this was no longer a flying visit, I thought it was time we had a talk."

"Anything in particular?"

He gave her a steady look. "We've managed to avoid each other for years, but since you're staying put, I thought it was important for us to clear the air."

"I guess we will see each other around a lot more," she hedged.

"It's unavoidable, unless that's what you'd prefer."

"Don't be silly. We're both adults now, and we've had other relationships. Besides, what we had was—"

An eyebrow shot up in that way he had as he waited for her to find the right words.

"We were kids," she said firmly. "Now, we can be friends again."

"Friends?"

He thought about that for a minute while she agonized over every word she'd spoken.

"I like the sound of that." He took a walk around the shop. "The place is looking better than it ever did."

"Thanks. Glitter and Gold was vacant for some time, as you no doubt are aware. The owners walked away without cleaning it up and it's been hard work. I hope it pays off."

"I'm sure it will. Poor Mr. Willis got sick real fast, and no one knew. It was a shame, but I'm glad you bought the place. Can I help at all?"

Maddie wasn't sure how she felt about him being

51

around. Could they really be friends now, even though he'd agreed to it? A lot of time had passed, so maybe it *was* possible. Like Ethan said, they couldn't avoid each other indefinitely. Not in a town as small as Maple Falls.

Chapter Seven

Maddie pointed at the walls she hadn't gotten to yet. "Can you paint?"

"Paint and anything else you need. Some people say I'm very handy. You know, I fixed up my parents' place after a maple branch fell on the roof. It looks okay and it's still standing."

"Good to hear." She looked at him thoughtfully. "What are you like at making shelves?"

"I could give it a go."

"Brilliant. Everyone else seems busy."

"Last resort, am I?" He grinned. "Don't answer that."

"I did notice that there is a lot of building going on," she said with a straight face.

Suddenly, he was serious. "Actually, that's true. Some of our residents aren't so happy about the type of building. Mickey Findlay's been trying to develop every square inch he can get his hands on and pressuring people into selling."

"That would ruffle some feathers."

"It has, plus it would be nice if Mickey looked at some

local firms before he brings in outsiders. Some have had to go work in Destiny."

"That's not right. I have heard some rumblings around town about it."

He shrugged. "I should have known, and I've probably bored you, but at least now you have another perspective."

"Coming from the law, I assume yours is a more valid one," she teased.

"Whoa. My opinion is my own. I'm just one man."

"A very important and influential one, so the gossip says."

He flushed a little. "I guess some people might be swayed by the voice of a sheriff, but I don't say what I think about political stuff to many people."

Now, it was her turn to be embarrassed. "I'm pleased you'd trust me enough."

"Always. Listen, I'd like to clear the air a little more, if you'll hear me out."

"I hoped we weren't going to be doing the whole awkward 'dance around each other' thing, but I'm not sure what else we have to talk about."

"It'd be nice to get some closure and move on."

Maddie wasn't sure that was necessary. "You want to do that now?"

"No time like the present, especially since we seem to be alone. That isn't going to happen much around here, as you know."

It was true: Maple Falls might be quiet, but being alone was a tricky thing to maneuver. "All right," she said tentatively. "You start."

He scrunched the brim of his hat a little and took a deep breath. "I'm sorry for how I reacted and all the things I said back then. When you told me you were leaving, I was shocked. You'd always said it would happen one day, so it wasn't your fault that I didn't choose to believe it. Whatever else happened, you were honest with me, and no one can ask for more than that. I should have said this long before this."

"Well, thank you for saying it now. I guess the angry young man from back then has finally been tamed." She gave him a wry smile.

"I might have been a bit slow at reading women at the time," he admitted. "Your turn."

Maddie couldn't believe they had got to this point in only a few minutes. Years ago, an acknowledgement, an understanding that her leaving was instrumental for her to reach her goal, was all she'd ever wanted from him. Now, here they were.

"I don't know what to say. You hurt my feelings when you doubted my reasons for leaving. You know what? None of it matters, because, like I said, we were kids. We grew up, and we know some stuff we didn't know before. Thanks for the apology, and I'm sorry too for my part in our break-up."

"It's not necessary. So, we're moving on?"

She nodded. "Look at us. We already have. Now, can you help with the shelves?"

"I can build and install them for you."

"I'm impressed."

He grinned. "I can't promise I'll be as good as the professionals, but hopefully you'll be pleased rather than surprised when you see them."

"You always had to be the best at what you did. I'm sure it's true in this case too. I'd like them over here."

As she showed him where the shelves would go, their conversation ran around inside her head. Her former boyfriend had filled out rather nicely from the gangly teen he used to be, and that wasn't the only change. Angry at her for leaving, and unwilling to discuss it civilly, they had avoided each other whenever she came home for the holidays or on a vacation. She'd heard how well he was doing. Caught glimpses of him morphing into the man he was today. People could change.

Had she been unfair to him? The truth of it smacked into her stomach like a mixer not fixed to the counter properly.

She took a deep breath. Like he said, it was time to clear the air. "I'm sorry that I waited so long to tell you I'd found a job and was staying in New York City. I can see now that I wanted the best of both worlds, because I didn't want to actually say goodbye."

"We really mucked things up back then, but we can move on," he grinned again, surer of himself than she had ever seen.

The uniform, a beige short-sleeved shirt, sat well on his broad shoulders, the black trousers a snug fit around his thighs. His badge gleamed, detracting slightly from the gun nestled in the holster on his hips. He was as handsome as a man could be. Ethan's sandy-colored hair might need a trim, but that and the hint of a shadow around his jaw only made him more appealing.

"I can come back after my shift and get started. Will you be here?"

She snapped out of her introspection with a blush. "Hah! I'm glued to the darn painting for the foreseeable future. You turning up like this was a good excuse for a break. I was about to make lunch. Would you like a sandwich?"

"If you have enough. What am I saying? The Flynn women always have heaps of food."

"That's because Ethan Tanner has hollow legs, and we never knew when you'd be around for a meal."

They both laughed as they headed out to the small garden. Maddie had set up a cooler and a trestle table so she could make sandwiches, and they had a place to eat. Plastic chairs that had been bought for the shop were in a stack. Ethan pulled them apart and helped her by buttering some bread while Maddie added the filling. Just as she finished, the Girlz piled out of the house with Big Red at their heels.

Suzy arrived first. "I smell coffee." She stated, before skidding to a stop when she saw Ethan.

This caused Angel and Gran to pile up behind her and Maddie grinned at their surprise. The most eligible bachelor in town surrounded by women was an interesting situation to witness.

"Hello, ladies." Ethan nodded at them.

Gran pushed between them. "Come on, Girlz. There's an apple and blackberry pie for after."

"We have to wait?" Ethan groaned, oblivious, or pretending to be, over the curiosity directed his way.

"You know how we do things, young man."

"Sorry, Mrs. Flynn. I don't know what I was thinking." He winked at the other women.

That broke the ice, and soon the Girlz were fussing over him. He was so good with people, natural and relaxed, and she remembered that children were his forte. Having seen him in action, Maddie guessed this was what made him such a good sheriff.

Even Big Red remembered him, it seemed. Wrapping himself around Ethan's legs, the cat head-butted his hand. Although he wasn't friendly with men in general, Big Red always classified Ethan as an exception. Her ex, Dalton, had been wary of the Maine Coon, and she had an inkling that her cat knew long before she did that the man was a schmuck.

"Still kicking around, boy?" Ethan rubbed the big head affectionately. "It seems like he's been around forever."

"He's not that old. I should know." Gran grinned as she piled a plate for him.

"I guess he's been away only as long as Maddie."

She let that be. She'd gotten Big Red from the shelter when she was in high school, and they had been almost inseparable ever since—apart from the time she was at college. After she'd moved to New York, whenever she came home for a week or more, Big Red had made the trip too.

She bit into a sandwich made with fillings from Gran's garden: fresh tomatoes, lettuce, pickles and topped with homemade mayonnaise. Ethan did the same, with a lot more fervor. His appetite certainly hadn't diminished. He polished off a few sandwiches and two slices of pie, washing it all down with two cups of coffee, while managing small talk with Gran and the other Girlz. Maddie found it fascinating to watch as they flirted and teased. It was like going back in time.

Finally, he stood up from the plastic chair and burped softly. "Excuse me. I hate to eat and run, but duty calls. Thanks for that delicious lunch and the delightful company." He bowed to the Girlz. "I'll see you tonight, Maddie."

Maddie returned his smile, feeling three more pairs of eyes on her. "See you then."

He'd barely made it through the shop when they swarmed her.

"Spill! Why is Ethan coming here tonight? Is it a date? That was fast," Suzy, principal of the local school, rattled off like a machine gun.

Maddie held up a hand to stop the bullets. "Don't be silly. He's coming to put up some shelves. The paint should be dry enough by tonight."

"Hmm. Is that all there is to it? You two used to be an item."

"It was a long time ago. Besides, I'm sure he has a girlfriend by now." Maddie willed her voice not to make it a question.

"No, he doesn't." Suzy gave her a searching look. "I'm pretty sure I told you that already."

"Did you? I don't remember."

The other women looked at her skeptically, but Maddie ignored them and began to clean up the lunch things.

Gran came to take the dishes from her. "Let me do that. I'm sure you have more important things to do."

She relinquished them, since it was true. Leaving her smirking friends behind was an added bonus. Even Gran appeared to be having fun at her expense.

"When I'm done here, I might head back to the house," Gran said. "I'm not climbing ladders and Big Red isn't happy that he's been left alone so much."

"I got that," Maddie said with a nod. "He's been very standoffish, even with me, because I keep sending him outside. He keeps getting in the way with his curiosity. Never mind. It'll all be over soon. I just hope he'll be happy here."

"He'll be happy wherever you are, sweetheart. That cat is like a big baby, and you're his momma who spoils him."

Maddie raised an eyebrow. "No one spoils him like you do."

Gran sniffed. "Well, I missed him nearly as much as I missed you."

She looked marginally guilty as she packed everything

into the basket. They both knew she'd been supplying Big Red a ridiculous number of treats despite Maddie's protests.

"Well, don't go feeding him any of these leftovers. In fact, leave the basket, and I'll bring it when I come home for dinner."

Gran gave Maddie her innocent look as she clipped a lead onto Big Red. "I wouldn't have."

Maddie shook her head and went back to painting the downstairs while the Girlz returned to sanding the walls upstairs, their laughter echoing behind them. Maddie had no doubt that the following conversation would be more about the sheriff than Big Red, and she was better off not knowing about it.

They could say what they liked. Ethan was being helpful, just like they were. No difference at all. And if one of her friends wanted to get better acquainted with him, that was none of her business either.

Chapter Eight

Maddie rushed home for the chicken salad Gran had made, then took a shower and tried to get the paint off her face. There was an awful lot of it and after scrubbing her skin until it was tender, she decided to tackle what was left tomorrow since she'd be bound to add to it. If it didn't come off, that didn't matter because Ethan wasn't coming to look at her.

With that in mind, she put the flowing skirt she'd intended to wear back in the closet and slipped on a spaghetti-strap mid-length dress. It was much more practical, but she hesitated before she left the room, checking herself in the floor-length mirror. Then she laughed at her reflection.

It was if she'd had a personality transplant since lunch, when all the reasons to keep not only Ethan but her thoughts of him at bay had slipped from her mind, replaced with how he looked and smelled so great, how kind and thoughtful he was. Apart from the fuss over her leaving, he'd always been that way and it was a shame that the bad things people did often hung around a lot longer than the good.

Determined, she said goodbye to Gran, who was packing a few of her endless possessions, something she'd started prior to Maddie's return, though strangely the place never seemed to get any emptier.

They'd have to get into some serious packing once the bakery was up and running. Maddie already felt bad Gran had used all her savings; the least she could do was make sure the apartment was comfortable, then help to get the house ready for sale. The problem with the latter was there were simply no spare minutes, let alone hours, despite Maddie working every day as long and hard as she could.

As she went out the front door onto the porch, something thumped her on the head. Big Red was sitting on the back of Gran's rocker taking the opportunity to remind her once more that she hadn't been paying him nearly enough attention to bat her with one of his hefty paws.

"Sorry, boy. Just a few more days, then we'll be settled in our own place and be together more often. It'll be better than New York, because you'll get to go outside whenever you feel like it. You saw the yard, which is just for you and me. You'll like it after I fix it up, I promise."

He turned his head away as if he didn't believe a word of it, so she kissed between his ears and left him to sulk. There wasn't much she could do about it and wanted desperately to believe he'd be happy living above the bakery. She also hoped he'd behave himself with her customers. He had enough personality for ten cats, and as many ideas for getting into trouble.

When she got to the store, she opened every window and door once more. The smell of paint was strong, and she worried that the fumes would linger after they'd finished their work. Nothing would be more off-putting in a bakery than the pungent odor of paint.

It wasn't until she reached the downstairs bathroom that she noticed glass on the floor. The window was smashed and ajar. She felt sure she'd closed it properly, but maybe not. The wind must have caught it and smashed it back against the sill.

After fetching the broom, she swept the shards into a pile. Just as she finished, she heard a car pull up out front. The door was open, and she could see through the window Ethan emptying his pickup. He'd already taken some of the wood and his tools out of the back, so she went and helped him carry the rest inside.

"You'll mess up your clothes," he warned.

"I could say the same to you."

"I'm dressed for this kind of work. You're not."

"I'm fine," she called behind her as she led the way out to the kitchen, where he placed everything on the floor beside the things she'd left there.

"What happened here?" He nodded at the pile of glass in the corner.

"A window got smashed. It must have been the wind."

"Would you show me which one?"

She pointed to the bathroom, a little disturbed over his deceptive casualness.

Ethan didn't take long. "You're probably right," he said as he looked around the kitchen. "Nothing looked touched or was missing?"

"I don't think so. Why do you ask?"

"Just ruling out a break-in."

"Thanks. Now I'll be paranoid." She looked around her. There was very little to entice a would-be burglar, unless they were after paint and the old sheets they'd used to protect the recently polished floors.

"Don't mind me. Being suspicious is a by-product of the job. Don't cut yourself on that." He pointed to the glass. "In fact, leave it, and I'll take it with my trash when I leave."

It was odd to have a man being so caring about her, and it did feel nice. Dalton had always called her independent, and she liked that she was, even though it had seemed like an excuse for him to be unromantic and selfish.

"Earth to Maddie."

Ethan was looking at her funny, and she realized he had still been speaking.

"Sorry. I was miles away. What did you say?"

"I asked if this wood is all right. I wasn't sure if you wanted to stain or paint it."

"I prefer painted shelves. I think they'll be easier to clean, and when I put the baskets of bread on them, they'll look really appealing."

"Then this will be fine, but I'm sure a shelf couldn't make your bread any more appealing. Your baking was awesome back in the day. I bet it's even better now."

Ethan had been her guinea pig, but that didn't mean much. "You would have eaten anything back then and I'm pretty sure you did."

He laughed. "It's kind of true, but don't sell yourself short. You're a great cook, and I believe you have some trophies to prove it?"

"One or two," she answered proudly.

Gran had always praised her, and she'd received plenty of kudos from her tutors and mentors. From Ethan, it made her feel awkward. That was silly, when they'd been friends for so long except for that one huge argument.

The distance had proven too great. Having no idea how

long she'd be gone or if she would ever come back, Ethan, had suddenly decided that this was all a surprise, and since he had no ambition to leave Maple Falls, had accused her of planning the end of their relationship all along.

She gave herself a mental shake to dispel those dark days. "Did you know it's a fact that people eat with their eyes first, so any help in that aspect is a good thing."

His eyes twinkled at her. "Which is why I'll have to watch myself and up my exercise if I'm going to set foot in your bakery after you open. If it's all right with you, I'll bring my tools into the kitchen in case any of the paint is still wet in the shop. There's bound to be a mess of sawdust."

"Anywhere you want is fine."

Maddie waited as he set up a couple of wooden sawhorses and a large saw. When it looked like he had everything under control and didn't need a spectator, Maddie took her laptop outside to avoid the noise and dust he was about to make.

She sat at the trestle table and began to type up some lists. They were a specialty of hers, much like a savory muffin or a chocolate brownie recipe. There was a list for the first batch of baking she would do, a shopping list for ingredients, and another for all the items required for baking, such as pans and utensils.

Gran was donating some of her "oldie but goodie" pans, and Maddie had a lot of her own that would be arriving on the truck any day, but there were several items she would still need, like tongs and paper bags, and since she was eventually going to have people eat in, she'd need plates and cutlery.

Camille had sent her a shop-opening present of two hundred cake/cookie boxes stamped with her logo: a rolling pin with the words Maple Lane Bakery, a name she and Gran had chosen because it sounded so right, across the middle. It was so cute, she had nearly cried. They were covered with an old sheet in the corner of the kitchen to keep them safe.

One item that headed her list had her worried. From years in the industry, she knew there was a great deal of money to be made in coffee—the latte/cappuccino kind—therefore, it was a necessity. It would also make the dining-in experience more appealing.

The problem was, when would she find the time to learn how to use a coffeemaker or interview potential baristas? Her experience with bakeries had been in the kitchen, or behind the counter, not making fancy coffees.

She kept Googling the machines to see if some were easier than others to operate and was so engrossed in studying the various kinds online that she wasn't aware of the sawing and hammering ceasing until Ethan appeared at the door. Hot and sweaty, with bits of sawdust stuck to his forearms and face, he looked fantastic.

She gulped. "How's it going?"

He rolled his shoulders, cracked his neck on both sides with a satisfied sound, and when his t-shirt stretched as far as it could across his biceps, she had to look away.

"All done."

"You've finished?" Maddie was shocked. She'd expected him to take a few evenings to complete the shelves.

"Sounds like you don't believe me. It's coming up toward nightfall. I guess you didn't notice, what with all that thinking and list-making going on." He nodded at her laptop.

She checked her watch and was astounded. Now that summer was approaching, the days were longer, and she had been oblivious to the sun setting. Another thing bothered her: he'd been here for three hours, working solidly, and she hadn't so much as offered him some water. "I'm a terrible host. Can I get you anything? A drink? Something to eat?"

He grinned. "I'm fine. I didn't think you'd mind me helping myself to water. Come see if they're what you had in mind."

She closed the laptop and followed him inside. The shelves were exactly where and how she wanted them. "Ethan, they're perfect. I can't believe you did all this in such a short time. They look professionally made."

"Darned if you don't make a compliment sound bad with all that disbelief around it."

"You know what I mean."

He gave her a wry smile. "You meant that as a sheriff, I did a reasonable job."

"Stop fishing for those compliments. They're awesome. Truly. Exactly what I wanted."

"Why, thank you. I've given them a sanding, so they should be okay to paint tomorrow after a quick wipe."

"I can't tell you how grateful I am, especially as this is probably one of your nights off. How much do I owe you?"

He held his hand up. "Let's say it's a 'welcome home' and housewarming present combined, since I'm glad you're back and that you're staying."

She flushed at such a gesture. "Don't be silly. It's too much. I hope you didn't think I expected it for nothing."

He shook his head, looking exasperated. "Maddie, just say thank you."

She hadn't meant to offend him, and she didn't want to turn this into an argument. "Thank you very much."

"You're *very* welcome. Now, I need a hot shower and a soft bed."

He looked tired, but that didn't stop her from envisaging him under running water then snuggling into a soft bed. At this rate, she might need a cold shower. What had gotten into her? She chastised her wild imagination as she helped him put his stuff in the pickup. Like the gentleman Ethan was, he waited while she locked up.

"Good luck with the rest of the painting. I probably won't see you for the next few days, but I'll be sure to come by when you're open."

She leaned in his open window. "When you do, lunch is on me. Make that several lunches."

"Be careful what you wish for." He tapped her on the nose, and when she backed up, he drove off with a cheeky wave.

Good advice. Yes, she'd better be careful. Ethan could eat up any profits in one sitting. She smiled at the idea.

"Still after him, I see."

Maddie jumped a foot. "Virginia. I didn't notice you there."

Her archenemy from school gave her a cool up and down appraisal.

"It's a free sidewalk, the last time I looked, and some of us like to keep fit."

Maddie had an urge to suck in her stomach despite being happy with her weight. "Working twelve hours or more a day, a lot of the time in hot temperatures, is enough exercise for me."

"Hmm. How we look is obviously more important to some of us than others."

The glint in Virginia's eyes was an indication of her

satisfaction that her barb had hit home. Somehow, it compelled Maddie to explain things.

"Actually, Ethan offered to do a job for me, and now that he's done, I'm about to head home."

Virginia did an imitation of having eaten something bad, and Maddie had to wonder at the woman's business sense. If she was going to be so nasty, she could kiss goodbye to the listing of Gran's place. Apparently, she didn't care.

"You know he's too good for you."

Maddie was amazed at the venom in that statement, and then it hit her between the eyes. Virginia was one more casualty to fall under Ethan's spell. Since college, Maddie had heard nothing about Virginia being with a man, and she'd made up her mind that the real estate agent didn't particularly like men. Or, for that matter, anyone. What if her dislike of Maddie was fueled by her desire for Ethan?

Whatever her motives, she didn't have to be so downright rude, and Maddie could hardly ignore what she'd said.

"For goodness' sake, we went out when we were teenagers. I'm not after a relationship with Ethan Tanner."

Virginia tilted her head. "Then, why is he spending every spare minute with you?"

Maddie sighed. "He's not. If you must know, today was the first time we've seen each other closer than a street away for years. He made me some shelves. That's what friends do for each other," she said, quoting him. "Anyway, why do you care who he spends his time with?"

The answering beet-red flush confirmed what Maddie had been thinking, and she couldn't help asking, "You like Ethan?"

Virginia's eyes narrowed. "What if I do?"

The admission, or lack of a refute, was too much for Maddie. "I see," was all she could muster.

"It's none of your business who I like or don't like," Virginia growled.

"That's true. Perhaps you could remember that the next time you want to attack me."

Virginia took a step closer. "You think you're so clever, but you'll get your due."

Maddie's eyes widened at the other woman's aggression. "Are you threatening me?"

"Whatever." Virginia gave her a withering glare and stormed off down Maple Lane.

Maddie went from anger to pity. That woman wouldn't be happy even if she won the lottery.

Shame she'd managed to spoil a wonderful day.

Chapter Nine

The day before the shop was to open, they were sitting in their new kitchen at the large counter where the prep work and pastry making would be done. It also served as a place to have their meals, which kept them from making a mess in the small kitchen upstairs.

Gran, who had been up early, went home and returned with one of her small packing boxes, which she placed in front of Maddie, then sat beside her with an expectant gaze.

"Did you want me to unpack this?"

Gran nodded. "Please."

"Right now?" They had a million and one things to do before tomorrow, and unpacking Gran's things wasn't on Maddie's "important" list. It was weighing on her mind that there was a fair bit of packing still to do at Gran's despite the hours that had already been devoted to it. Maybe this was a subtle hint to do more.

Gran was trying not to grin. "Go ahead. I think you'll find them useful."

Intrigued, Maddie cut the tape and reached into the box to pull out something carefully wrapped in newspaper. She placed it on the counter and unwrapped it, revealing one of Gran's cups from her English china collection. Small white daisies graced the blue sides.

"I don't understand."

"You don't have to use them, but with the English theme you have going in the store, I think they'd suit things very well."

She was referring to the pale blue and white colors, which was reminiscent of the famous willow pattern on some English crockery.

"I absolutely love the idea, but what if they get broken?"

Gran shrugged. "I'm not bothered. They were made to be used."

This was a change of tune. Gran had collected the cups and saucers all her life. For her to suddenly decide that it didn't matter if they broke, when Maddie had been told to be careful since she was old enough to have her own set, was strange. And yet, Gran had never hidden them away, only to be brought out on special occasions. Everything she owned was used as often as it was needed. Her generosity was limitless.

"If you really don't mind, I'd love to use them. Thank you, and I'll be as careful as I can."

"Good. That's settled. I have the Girlz coming in an hour, and they're bringing the rest of them. Laura has Noah and Bernie bringing my cabinet, and I thought we could put it in the corner by the display cabinets, so the plates can be reached when someone orders tea."

"Your cabinet? Laura?"

"Yes. Without all the sets, the cabinet is redundant at my place. Besides, after all this time they belong together. As for Laura's involvement, she felt awful about not helping before this, but you know how bad her allergies are."

"I wasn't even aware of them until Angel told me."

Gran frowned. "It's such a shame, but you can't help that sort of thing, can you? Poor girl."

It felt odd to be talking about Laura helping when Maddie was so sure that Laura disliked her. "It's very kind of everyone. Especially you, with the cabinet and the china. You're getting kind of sneaky," she teased.

Gran giggled like a naughty child. "I know, and it feels good. Let's start baking for tomorrow and give our guests a treat for helping us."

"Great idea. We can be testing this fancy new oven at the same time."

When everyone arrived, they were taking out the last of four cakes.

Maddie called out to them. "Come in, everyone. Your timing is perfect."

Suzy put a box on the counter, which was clean again after their baking session. "The smell is divine."

Angel's eyes glittered with unconcealed desire when she saw the cakes cooling. "I hope there's some for us."

"The place looks amazing." Laura had come through the door, leading Noah the town yoga instructor, and Bernie, who were hauling Gran's china cabinet. They were fit enough, but the cabinet weighed a ton, as Maddie knew from having helped move it when Gran had a dusting spree twice a year.

Gran tutted, as she often did when things went awry. "You should have used the front door, boys. But never mind. You're here now, and the doorways inside are generous."

Which proved to be just as well, as the back door was definitely a struggle, and the men broke into a sweat as they cajoled the cabinet through and into the kitchen. Finally, it was inside the shop, and Maddie was happy to let Gran dictate where it went. They all stood back to admire the effect.

Angel ran to the kitchen and returned with two of the tea sets that had been unwrapped. She placed them on the middle shelf.

Gran sniffled, and they turned as one, full of concern. She waved them back. "I'm being silly."

Maddie wrapped an arm around her slight shoulders. "It's not silly if it upsets you. We can take them back home or repack them. There's absolutely no need to have them in the shop."

Noah and Bernie groaned at the idea of moving the cabinet again.

Gran laughed. "I'm not upset. I think they look so darn perfect in here, in your shop. It's seeing your dream come alive that's making me feel this way."

Maddie shook her head with relief, biting back her own tears, as were the Girlz, while the men shuffled their feet.

"They do look good, don't they?" she managed.

"Perfect, just like Gran said." Angel wiped the corners of her eyes.

Before things could get any more awkward, Gran clapped her hands as if she were herding young children. "Enough. This is a happy time. Into the kitchen with you all. A cup of tea and some cake will fix us women up nicely for the work ahead, and you boys deserve a treat for carting that cabinet so far."

"Sorry, I can't stay. My shift at O'Malley's is about to start." Laura headed for the back door.

"That's a shame, but thanks for organizing them to bring the cabinet. It was a lovely surprise."

Laura gave Maddie a weak smile. "You're welcome. See you all later."

The men were practically salivating at the thought of sampling the fresh baking. Suzy and Angel hastily unwrapped enough cups and saucers, and Noah and Bernie watched excitedly as Maddie frosted a large chocolate cake.

She brought it to the table, laughing at their expressions until she noticed the men regarding the small finger holds on the dainty cups with dismay. That made her laugh harder. "I guess we didn't think it through. Would you rather have a mug? Or you can have coffee, if you prefer."

Bernie grinned with relief. "You're a star, Maddie. Coffee, please. In a mug."

Gran tutted but made them coffee. Because she was a devout tea drinker, she often forgot that most Americans preferred coffee. It was lucky that Maddie had already purchased mugs.

It was luckier still that she had such good friends. The place would soon be ready for tomorrow. The only nagging issue was she still had no barista or any other help other than Gran, which wouldn't do on an ongoing basis. This was not how she wanted things to be since she was usually so organized.

As Gran often said, it was far better to dwell on the good things, and several of them were right in front of her, eating the rich chocolate cake as if they were eating for the first time and loving every mouthful.

She couldn't be happier.

Chapter Ten

Maddie smoothed down her clean white apron and turned the sign to OPEN. She wasn't sure what to expect from the first day. She'd done little to advertise her bakery apart from an ad in the local paper and flyers in the other shops which the Girlz had delivered. Time simply hadn't been on her side, and without Gran's help in the kitchen, she wouldn't have had any hope of opening today.

Determined not to dwell on what she hadn't done, especially when ironically she'd advised clients in her previous job against rushing, she went outside to admire the new sign in the window and then the sandwich board which stood proudly on the pavement close to the road.

"Maple Lane Bakery," she said aloud, enjoying the sound of it. Right here in front of her was her living dream. Her eyes prickled, and she had to swallow hard to keep herself from bawling like a baby.

Smiling at her silliness, she opened the door, and the tinkle of the bell welcomed her. Satisfied, she went and stood behind the counter, trying not to look too eager.

Something caught her eye, and she turned to find Big Red looking around the doorway from the kitchen.

"That wasn't the dinner bell, boy," she said affectionately to the big feline, who was still coming to terms with two changes of address in as many months. "You'd better head back before I get into trouble with the health department."

She'd explained things to him several times, and he seemed to have understood most of it, but today he'd been underfoot, demanding attention as if he knew something was unfolding. With a haughty wave of his tail he went through the kitchen and outside.

Recently, he'd laid claim to a nice spot under the hedge, and whenever he was sent out of the kitchen, that was his sulking hideout. He would look at her working at the kitchen sink, from under the branches, with displeasure and was usually successful in his endeavors to make her feel guilty.

Maddie sighed and followed at a distance, just to be sure. There would be people who'd be delighted to point out the health issues with having an animal on the premises, and she didn't want to invite any trouble. Poor Big Red.

Used to having his freedom to wander at will, he was initially confused about the invisible line between the apartment and the shop, but today was the first time he'd ventured past the kitchen. He had taken to sitting in the kitchen doorway, watching with what she had decided was his "interested" expression as they put the shop together.

Several people walking down Plum Lane or coming to drop off supplies had made the mistake of trying to befriend him, but Big Red was the master of feline put-downs. He would hunch his back and fluff himself up as if he was about to attack. He never had, but they didn't know that, and didn't seem to believe Maddie's assurances, which was probably just as well.

The bell rang again, and when she pushed through the curtain she'd had installed to keep out flies, she saw Angel sweeping in.

If ever a name suited a person, it was hers. Tall and slim, with shoulder-length blonde hair, she was elegant and gorgeous. It was a good thing they were the best of friends, because a girl could get jealous of someone like her. That Angel had the personality of a saint helped immensely.

"My first customer," Maddie said with a grin.

"Naturally, sugar. I've been waiting for the last ten minutes so I could be."

"That's so sweet. Let me guess. A jelly doughnut?"

"You know me too well," Angel chuckled.

Maddie carefully bagged the doughnut and handed it to Angel. "Don't think about payment. The first one is free."

"You won't make your fortune if you give all your food away."

"One doughnut won't break the bank." It wouldn't make the bank, either. She'd need to sell all her stock every day for the next month to get her head even slightly above water, but today was special, and so was Angel.

Angel hesitated, but Maddie wouldn't take no for an answer.

"All right. Just this once." Angel took a stroll around the shop. "I see you have all Gran's teapots as well as the cups and saucers."

"To be honest, I'm worried about using them, but Gran insists they should be treated the same as her crockery. She hasn't had a lot of say in things apart from the name, so I agreed."

"It's a theme, and I think people will love it. If you can get them to change from coffee, that is."

The bell rang again, and Angel gave Maddie a wink and left with a small wave as Maddie served the couple who'd entered.

They weren't from Maple Falls—at least she didn't recognize them—and took some time choosing what they wanted. They raved about her selection, the shop, and the smells.

"Oh my, everything looks heavenly. I wish I could taste everything," the woman said.

"Let's get a few, and we can share," the man agreed.

Maddie boxed up their selection, taking this as a good sign from her first paying customers. She had just finished when her next customers arrived. After that, she was run ragged for a few hours. Gran helped out with teas and filtered coffees, delivering them with a smile and a bit of conversation. It seemed that everyone in town was taking the time to come by.

Eventually, the line out the door thinned, and Maddie managed a break to have a drink and catch her breath. Gran had already made her several cups of tea, all of which had gone cold. Finally, she had the chance to enjoy one. She sipped with her eyes closed, a smile on her face. She was surprised she could even work her lips and cheek muscles, thanks to all the smiling she'd done that day, but she couldn't be happier. She was tired, no doubt about it, but happy.

Gran finished serving and came out to the kitchen where Maddie sat at the table, her feet up on a chair.

"You've done so well, sweetheart, but getting up at 3 a.m. to bake and stock the shelves, as well as running the shop until late afternoon, isn't something you can do every day. I'd hate to see you make yourself ill over this."

"It had to be done and I'm more concerned about you. I've tried so hard to find help. The ad in the local paper didn't turn up anyone I could use. Angel called me fussy, which is true, but this means a lot, and I don't want someone who doesn't love the process of baking or dealing with customers. It seems like we can have one or the other, but not both."

Gran nodded. "I did see the applicants' names, and I'm inclined to agree for the most part, but sometimes you have to take what you can get."

The bell chimed, and Maddie jumped up from the chair, grateful for the interruption on an issue she couldn't see the answer to.

"Hi, Denise," she greeted her visitor with pleasure.

The mayor was a generously proportioned woman who was loved by the town. Not only did she give all she had to help make it a beautiful and safe place to live, she was also incredibly kind.

"Hi, Maddie, and congratulations! You've worked your butts off, getting this place up and running."

"Thanks. You look like you've been working too hard as well?"

Denise was quite pale. The deep blue of her suit jacket didn't help.

"I am a little tired, which is why I haven't been around. I wondered if I was coming down with something, but I had a meeting in town, so I couldn't pass by the shop and not come in."

"I hope you feel better soon. We appreciate you stopping by." Gran had gone around the counter, and by the keen interest she was showing appeared close to giving Denise an exam.

The mayor grinned. "I'm fine, really, and nothing happens in my town I don't know about, even if I'm only making a flying visit."

"So, you won't be buying anything?" Maddie teased.

"Are you kidding? You forget I've eaten more of your food than anyone except for Angel and Suzy. I can and will endorse every mouthful, but only if I've tried it. Plus, I didn't get these curves from saying no to a chocolate croissant. Or two."

They were laughing hard when in walked the person most likely to give anyone indigestion. Virginia. Her real estate business was at the fancier end of Maple Lane, and everything about her was fake except for her meanness. Still, she was a customer. Maddie replaced the smile that had slipped, hoping it didn't look as forced as it felt.

"Virginia, how are you?" Denise asked in her friendly way.

"Still sugar dependent, Mayor?"

Maddie could have thrown a cream pie at her, but Denise was a professional and wouldn't rise to the bait.

"When it's Maddie who made it, who wouldn't be? What are you getting?"

"Me?" Virginia looked horrified. "I don't eat this kind of food."

Everyone in town knew how Virginia was, but it still made Maddie angry that she couldn't try to be nicer. It wouldn't kill the woman.

"Then, what did you want?" she asked coolly.

"It's a private matter. When can I see you, Mayor? Your secretary said you were in a meeting when I called, and then I saw you come in here."

Her disdainful look might have made other people quail, but Denise stood as tall as she could and walked to the door. "My meeting was down the road, and I hope you wouldn't deny me a lunch break. If it's urgent, make an appointment for later today."

Maddie admired everything about Denise these days. Unfortunately, Virginia did not. As soon as the mayor had disappeared, she rounded on Maddie.

"Our mayor is getting far too uppity."

"Denise? I don't think so."

"Of course you'd stick up for her. All of you in your group are just as bad."

While she was capable of keeping an even temper when Virginia maligned her, Maddie wasn't about to let her badmouth the Girlz. "Friends are like that. Wouldn't you agree?"

Virginia glared at her and was about to say something when she apparently thought better of it. Instead, she wheeled around on her very high heels and left, slamming the door behind her, making the glass rattle in its frame.

Maddie hadn't liked the look on her face as she left. She shouldn't have insinuated that Virginia didn't have friends, subtly or not. An enemy like Virginia wasn't something she intended to cultivate, but it was sometimes difficult to turn the other cheek in the face of such contempt.

The afternoon went much slower, and Maddie was thinking that her 3:30 closing time might be a stretch, when just after 3 o'clock, Layla Dixon came in with Jessie and James, her twin boys. Layla was the nurse for the local doctor and Ethan's sister. They had become close during their teenage years because of him, but Layla was a genuinely nice woman.

The boys were loud and fast. Darting around the shop

while Maddie and Layla chatted, they almost succumbed to touching the muffins as they lifted a mesh dome on the counter.

"Keep your grubby hands to yourselves, both of you," Layla growled at her towheaded darlings.

"But, Mom, we're starving." James gripped his stomach, doing an impression of someone who hadn't eaten for days.

"You're always starving." Layla sighed at their pitiful looks. "All right. Choose one thing each."

"Aww, just one thing?" Jessie had his face pressed against the glass display case.

"One or none. And get your face off that glass now, mister."

They dithered back and forth between the selections, jumping up and down in front of the displayed doughnuts, croissants, buns, cupcakes, and cookies.

Layla sighed again. "This could take a while."

"They're fine," Maddie waved a hand. "Don't worry about it. It's been a while since we've talked. How's work?"

"Being the only practice in town, the place is always busy. Luckily for me, Dr. Liston had a seminar this afternoon, so I was able to finish early. I thought I'd surprise the boys by picking them up from school and treating them. How did your first day go?"

"Fantastic. The case was full, and this is all I have left."

"You sound pretty relieved."

"I am. Can you imagine if I hadn't sold anything?"

Layla laughed at her expression. "That, I can't do. Everyone loves your food. It couldn't happen."

Before Maddie had time to deal with her embarrassment, Ethan came through the door. He put his hand on the old-fashioned bell so it made no sound as he crept up behind the boys to grab the backs of their necks. He gave them a little shake, and, far from being scared, his nephews went crazy. They loved their uncle, who, Maddie had been told by the Girlz, was very hands-on. Clearly, that was true.

"The place looks amazing," he said. "Just how you described it."

Everyone's attention going elsewhere meant Maddie's pink cheeks had a chance to return to normal before anyone could notice. Layla's praise was enough to make her blush, without the help of Ethan's comments. Darn it.

Angel had told her that Ethan felt sorry his sister was a single mom, but he loved these boys as if they were his own. Maddie had always hated being an only child, and she envied Ethan and Layla's closeness.

Exasperated by the noise, Layla rounded up the twins, made them choose their treats, which happened to be the same chocolate cupcake, then herded them out the door with a promise of a visit to the park.

When they were gone, Ethan gave Maddie a wry grin. "Those boys are a handful."

Maddie scoffed. "What boys aren't? Big or small."

"True. Hey, are you making a dig at me?"

"Well, you did start all that hyperactivity," she teased.

His blue eyes twinkled. "I don't know what you mean. Can I have a dozen buns and half a dozen croissants, please? Oh, and you'd better add six cupcakes."

She raised an eyebrow. "Stocking up?"

"I may have a big appetite for delicious things, but Layla invited me to dinner. The least I can do is take more food. Jessie and James have hollow legs, but with a little luck, there'll be enough left for their school lunches tomorrow."

She put everything else into paper bags, then boxed up the cupcakes while he quietly waited. It was hard to be aloof when a man who looked like Ethan was standing barely two feet away and watching your every move.

He was so much more than her ex-boyfriend. Gone was the young man who hadn't a clue what to do with his life. He was the sheriff, one who fostered good community relations, according to Angel. He was also thoughtful, and a great uncle and brother. He'd be a good catch. If she was fishing.

"I thought I wouldn't see you for a while," she said, tucking the lid down.

"There's been a lot going on lately, which is keeping me busy, but I was down the road at the park looking over the setup for the spring festival on Saturday, so I thought I'd come by and see how your first day went."

"I was telling Layla I'm really happy with it. Knock on wood, it'll be a continuing trend."

"I'm so happy for you. Hey, speaking of the fair, I was going through the list of vendors, and I noticed you aren't running a stall. Wouldn't it be a good opportunity for the business?"

"I know it would have helped get the word out, but I decided against it. With the opening this week, it would have been crazy to attempt it. Actually, I'm so glad I already made the decision because I haven't had a spare minute. Getting the place ready and all the baking that had to be done, a stall would have sent me right over the edge."

"We can't have that. I hear you still have no staff other than Gran. Will you be at the festival at all?"

She nodded. "I wouldn't miss it. I'm not opening on weekends until I can find some help, so I entered the apple pie competition."

"I'm glad to hear you're not working seven days. You

don't want to overdo things. I hear owning your own business can be very stressful." He winked at her.

"And very rewarding. Today was awesome, but I really hope somebody replies to my ad soon."

"Is there anything I can do?"

Maddie heard the sincerity in his voice, but she couldn't suppress a laugh. "Last I heard, you burn toast on a regular basis."

He grinned back. "I've come a long way from that. Layla still feeds me several times a week, but I've perfected a few dishes."

"Really?"

"Okay, 'perfected' may be an exaggeration, but they're edible. Especially when you're starving. And there's nothing else available."

"I think I'll keep looking, but thanks for the offer. Anyway, I'm closing soon. Mid-afternoon is long enough for now. I'm looking forward to a rest and recharging the batteries."

"Good for you." He held out some money.

She jumped back. "No way am I taking that. Call it payment for the shelves."

"This is far too much. I don't want to eat up your profits."

She couldn't help smiling at the pun. "Those few bags are nowhere near enough. Besides, like I said, I'm closing soon. Nearly everything I have left will go in the trash."

"Wow." Ethan studied the display case once more. "I'd love to talk to you about that sometime. We have a group in Maple Falls who collect food for the needy. They'd jump at the chance to share your baking."

Maddie nodded enthusiastically. "I'd be interested. The

last place I worked donated their day-end food the same way. It's such a great cause."

"Awesome. We can organize a time soon. I'll see you Saturday, if not before."

As she watched him leave, Maddie realized the sense of awkwardness was slowly fading. Maybe you really could be friends with old flames.

Chapter Eleven

Saturday dawned sunny and hot, and was even hotter by mid-morning, when Maddie parked Honey in the lot she'd heard Mr. Findlay wanted to buy. It would be a shame to lose it, since the space was necessary for the town's field days, festivals, and all the community events that were held on the adjacent grounds.

Stalls had been set up with their goods, and Maddie couldn't help a twinge of regret about not making the effort to run one, even knowing that the time factor had made it impossible. Word of mouth was a powerful tool and many of the visitors today would be from out of town.

Exhausted from her first week and worried this was all too much for her grandmother, she was still determined to enjoy the day.

She stretched, appreciating being out in the fresh air. Getting up a little later this morning had worked wonders, and with just one pie to make, she'd managed to put a lot of love into it. The basic recipe was Gran's, with a few special additions of her own.

She found the tent for the competitions and space on

the already loaded table for her entry. She was delighted with the golden color of the pastry (a trick Gran had inherited from her British mother) and the aroma as she pulled the pie from the box. Giving it a light dusting of confectioner's sugar she carefully placed it on a glass stand which also belonged to Gran.

Angel arrived and sighed when she saw Maddie's entry. "Your apple pie looks fantastic with those maple leaf decorations. I bet it's the best one here."

"Thanks. It's mostly Gran's recipe," Maddie admitted fondly.

"In that case, you're bound to win."

Maddie put a finger to her lips. "Shhh. We don't want to prejudice the judges."

Angel looked around. "They're too far away to hear me." She licked her lips. "I wish I could bake like you."

Those words always gave Maddie a buzz, especially when they came from her friends. "You're never too old to learn." She meant it sincerely.

Angel looked doubtful, as always, but seemed more eager than ever. "Do you really think so? I'd sure like to be able to cook something decent for a change."

Maddie couldn't imagine not being able to cook. To her, it wasn't just her job; she truly loved it and found she relished her ability to be creative. The bonus with using tried and true recipes was she had time to think and plan. Dough was the best for this multi-tasking, but most of her personal recipes were so familiar to her they required little thought.

The key ingredient was the pound or two of love she put into everything she baked. Doing so made her incredibly happy, and happier still to share that with her customers and friends.

Sharing that love and creativity on another scale was an idea which would not go quietly. Out of her mouth came the one thing she'd resisted for years. The one thing that, especially now, she didn't have time for. "I can give you a few lessons if you like."

Angel did a happy dance which wouldn't have been out of place in a Pink video. "That would be wonderful. Let me know when you can manage it."

What could Maddie do in the face of such enthusiasm? "It'd have to be in the evening."

"An evening would be perfect. I'm so excited! My mom wasn't a great cook, as you know. I learned very young how to heat noodles, and it's still the sad extent of my repertoire."

Maple Falls had its very own Pollyanna. Angel was never depressed or angry about her upbringing in a rundown trailer park or the failure of her teenage marriage to the captain of the football team, who turned out to be an all-around loser.

"I'm sure we can do better than that. I can't believe you still eat pots of noodles and look like you do," Maddie teased.

Angel had the figure of a siren and the classic good looks to match. Maddie had been a skinny kid, but baking and time had produced curves that weren't unwelcome. Still, she wasn't in Angel's category.

"I'll do anything if I can stop eating salad or takeout every night, and if you can teach me, you'll deserve a medal." Angel slapped her forehead. "Oh, wait, you already have one. And a degree. Teaching should be a piece of cake for you."

Maddie groaned at Angel's jokes, but inside she was pleased and upset in equal measure at being reminded of her scholarship and her subsequent business degree. The awards from competitions she'd entered over the last couple of years had gone a long way toward restoring her pride, but she still worried about people's reaction to her change of career. The degree had been a big help in setting up the business and she hoped everyone would appreciate that fact like she did.

Thanks to Gran's ability and enthusiasm, she'd always loved to bake, so all she had to do was find a pastry chef willing to give her an apprenticeship. Without Camille's help, she never would have had the opportunity to work in the family-run French bakery in New York City.

She liked to think she'd repaid the chance she'd been given. Working hard had paid off in a lot of ways, and as sorry as she'd been to leave Camille and her family, what she had now was the pinnacle of her career.

The feeling of achievement filled her over and over again, and she could see her friends' pride in her. She was darn proud of them, too.

"How's the salon going?" she asked Angel. "You always seem to be full."

"I shouldn't complain, but I'm too busy. I need another person, but you know yourself how hard it is to get help. So many people have been raving about your shop. Even the Blue Brigade have to admit your baking is the best."

Maddie laughed at Angel's description of the women from the country club who felt compelled to dye their hair varying shades of blue in imitation of their president. "That's good to hear, and it's everything I imagined. Having the shop with an apartment upstairs saves so much time. Gran and I have even been doing our own cooking down in the bakery, so the apartment kitchen stays nice and clean.

I've managed to plant some herbs, tomatoes and lettuce in the garden, too."

"Good grief, I'm feeling faint at the idea of doing all that. My flower beds are low maintenance and enough for these hands. I'm looking forward to when you get the coffee machine up and running. I'd love a latte to go with any of those delicious cakes you make."

"Arrgh! Don't remind me. That's the one thing I can't master. People have been great settling for ordinary coffee or a cup of tea, but I see the way they look at the machine. It's like an elephant in the room."

"We could put up a sign in my window advertising the job."

"That'd be great. How about I put up one for you? There must be someone who wants a job." Maddie stole a look around the tent, which was almost filled to capacity. "The judges are going to find it tough to decide anything today. There's some great food on display."

"All this talk of food is making me hungry. I need to buy something." Angel frowned. "Where's Gran today? She's never missed the fair, as far as I know. I usually grab some of her jam and pickles."

"She has an upset stomach, so she's gone to her place to do some more packing if she feels up to it. And she's been too busy baking to do any preserves this time."

"What a shame. When she enters something, it wins every time. You know, there must be a bug in town. I've heard of a few people with stomach problems."

Now Maddie was worried. "Really? Gran hasn't felt right since yesterday, and I was glad for her we weren't baking today. I thought it was getting better. Maybe I shouldn't have left her, but you know how she refuses to go to the doctor unless she's desperate."

"There you go, then. I'm sure it's the same as what the others have had, but if she's not okay soon, maybe a trip to the doctor wouldn't hurt."

"I'm definitely going to drag her there if she's not better by tomorrow." Maddie was only half-joking.

"Give her my love, and I'm sorry she's missing all the fun. Let's meet for lunch before the judging."

"I thought you were going to buy something to eat?"

"I can do both. After all, it's only mid-morning."

Angel grinned and sauntered off, which made Maddie laugh as she strolled around the stalls. It was one of those things she'd missed doing, along with all the other festivals Maple Falls had going on during the year. It was also a chance to catch up with people she hadn't seen for a while.

Chapter Twelve

N oah Jackson was positioned on a roped-off grassy area, giving a free yoga class for novices. He had quite a crowd. Then again, Noah was a very nice sight and one of the few men who looked good in Lycra. His shoulder-length, almost black hair was tied in a ponytail and was suited just as well to his other job as the local DJ.

"Maddie!" Mick from the second-hand store had a stall nearby, and he beckoned her over. "I was saving this for Gran, but I hear she's not feeling her best today. Do you think she'd like it, or is she not collecting anymore, since you have most of her things in the shop?"

From years of following Gran's passion, Maddie knew instantly the teapot he was holding was a Royal Albert. With delicate pink flowers and a pink lower half, it was lovely.

"It's gorgeous, and I know she'd love it. I don't know if she'll collect to the same extent, since she's selling the house." Maddie tipped it over to check the price and saw Mick didn't want an arm and a leg for it. "Still, I think I'll take it as a surprise for her. It may make her feel a little better."

"Excellent." He wrapped it up and put it in a bag. "Good luck with the pie, although I figure you won't need it."

"Thanks, Mick."

She wandered through the stalls, those whose owners had been coming for decades as well as those who were new, which carried all the usual crafts and bric-a-brac. All around her, children were bobbing for apples and enjoying the rides and sideshows. The smells of cotton candy, fudge, and toffee apples mingled with those of hot dogs, pickles, and cheeses.

She inhaled deeply and found herself at Janet Mitchell's stall. Stacks of amazing looking fresh vegetables were the envy of everyone since she grew most of them herself. Her variety of herbs had Maddie wishing she could buy them, but she wasn't making too many savory things yet, and she'd just planted some in her own garden.

She waved and walked on. Everyone was pleasant, enjoying the weather and the fun, and her shoulders lost a lot of their tension. When she made her way to the lunch tent, Suzy, Angel and Laura were already there.

Suzy stood and offered Maddie her chair. "I can't stay. I had a quick bite, but I've got some more things to announce before they start the judging." Suzy, wearing her principal mantle, was MC for the day. She had the perfect voice for it and was cuteness personified. With her dark hair and skin, and warm chocolate eyes, she could get a person to do anything she asked without much effort.

As Suzy left, Maddie looked around. "Where's Denise?"

"Didn't you see the tables she has to judge?" Angel

asked. "She'd been tasting for hours, and there's still a way to go."

"Of course. Poor Denise, if she's not feeling too good, that's the last thing you want to be doing. It'd actually be a perfect job for you, Angel."

Angel winked. "I was thinking the same thing. Maybe next year. Although how I'd stop at one bite, I can't imagine."

"I read that it's one of the mayor's jobs," Laura said.

Maddie frowned. "I'm sure it's not written in stone."

Laura crossed her arms. "Maybe not, but the town seems to be pretty fixed on certain things."

"That's true." Angel nodded at Maddie's bag. "What did you buy?"

"Something for Gran. What do you think?"

Maddie carefully showed the Girlz the teapot, wondering if Angel was trying to diffuse the awkward atmosphere between her and Laura, which had come out of nowhere as far as Maddie was concerned.

Laura was quiet while they ate their club sandwiches and drank the lattes Angel had bought and listened to Suzy's voice explaining over the loudspeakers what was happening at any given time.

The speakers crackled once more.

"Could all contestants for the baking competition return to the tent? The judges have made their decisions. Our mayor is the lead judge for cakes, pies, and cookies. Isaac Carter from the diner is the same for savory dishes, and Noah Jackson is judging pickles and preserves."

They went through to the main tent, and Maddie moved to the back while Angel and Laura stayed closer to the judges.

Most people cheered as the winners were announced. It

was a slow process for them to collect their trophies and certificates as there were a lot of categories. Maddie would have to endure a long wait, since pies were at the end of the list.

A group from Maple Falls country club was standing close to the small stage. They were looking at the judges, but one or two of them sent a scowl Maddie's way. The president, Maude Oliver, known for her stage whispers, uttered something to her friends that was loud enough for the entire crowd to hear.

"She's a professional from New York City. It's absolutely unfair she was allowed to enter."

"She could have been a judge, not a contestant," her co-conspirator, Irene Fitzgibbon agreed.

Maddie started looking for an escape route just as Angel, who was only a few feet away from the women, joined in the discussion.

"Maybe next time she'd agree to do that, but since the judges were decided upon months ago, before Maddie decided to come home and open the bakery, it shouldn't be an issue, and it's hardly her fault. Is it?"

Angel winked again, and Maddie hid an answering smile. She followed her friend's nod to an opening at the back of the tent, and they met outside.

"Thanks for sticking up for me," Maddie said. "You were there at the perfect time."

"Hey, that's what friends are for. I saw them circling, and I heard the rumbles long before that. I thought it was my stomach at first, but it turned out to be something a lot more sinister. Besides, the president of our country club should have better manners and not be so rude."

"She should, but I guess they have a point. Baking is what I do for a living, after all."

Angel shrugged. "Most of them don't work, so for all we know, it could be something they're doing all day."

Angel's logic was a beautiful thing.

"You know, I was worried the three of us would lose something as we got older," Maddie said. "With me first at college, then working in New York. But it feels exactly the same. I've missed you and Suzy and our crazy sweet town."

"And Laura," Angel said automatically. "We missed you too, but I don't know why you think anything could change between us. Girlz forever, that's us four."

Maddie felt a lump grow in her throat, despite the addition of Laura. "I always hoped it wouldn't change. There were a couple of horrible people in New York City who started out nice, and it did worry me."

Angel looked pointedly back at the tent. "I don't think New York City or anywhere else has a monopoly on horrible people. Did you not see the Blue Brigade?"

Maddie laughed. "How could I miss those looks? Or the barbed comments, even though they tried to be quiet about it?"

Angel snorted. "They couldn't be quiet about anything if their lives depended on it. They've got an opinion on everything, including Denise's fall from grace."

Maddie frowned. "I heard from Bernie about her being harassed, but she hasn't said a thing about it, so I figured it was a storm in a teacup."

"You know Denise, she rolls with the punches, and lately I haven't heard much in the salon, so maybe it has all died down."

"I hope so, because I noticed she doesn't look too well."

"Hah! If you had to try all those pies and cakes, you'd be feeling a little off too. Especially the ones which aren't really edible." Angel said it straight-faced, but her eyes twinkled.

Maddie laughed. There had been some truly horrid looking cakes, and she didn't envy Denise having to taste each one.

"Would it make a difference to you, as long as it was cake?" she teased.

Angel pushed her gently. "How rude. I have a very discerning palate."

"Since when?"

They were nearly on the ground with laughing so hard when Ethan came around the corner of the tent. He studied them for a minute as they tried to get themselves together.

"The judges are ready for the grand finale. If you're interested, I hear a certain apple pie has everyone excited."

A shiver went down Maddie's spine. She was definitely interested—she'd been entering competitions since she was a kid, yet she always got this same thrill. "We'll be right in."

After he'd gone, Angel gave her another little push. "Did you see the way he looked at you?"

Maddie waved her away. "He was looking at you too."

Her friend's eyes twinkled. "He knows I'm divorced and happy to stay that way."

"Good point, but it doesn't stop a man from looking."

Angel put her arm through Maddie's. "You're such a cynic."

"Maybe a little jaded. When you've been cheated on, it tends to tarnish your belief in men altogether." She and Angel had both been attached to scumbags who had treated them badly, and Maddie wasn't sure why that meant she was expected to get back in the dating market if Angel wasn't. In fact, Angel had been single a lot longer.

Angel frowned. "You're preaching to the choir. Still,

we'll have to work on that for you. You know, Ethan's about as good as it gets around these parts. Anyway, let's get in there. I really need some food."

They ducked through the tent flap, and Maddie stood at the back of the eager crowd while Angel peeled off.

Suzy came to stand beside her. "Where's Angel?"

"Probably hovering by the homemade fudge. That woman has the worst sweet tooth in town. Lucky for her, she's got the best metabolism in the world. And, no, I'm not at all resentful."

They smothered their laughter as the judges prepared to open the last envelope. Maddie felt unease slip through her when she noticed Laura standing next to the group of women who had been so scathing earlier. When Laura saw her watching, she disengaged herself a little too quickly for Maddie's liking.

Laura had become Angel's friend after Maddie left for New York. Maddie hoped the feeling of animosity she got from Laura when they were alone was just in her head and wasn't some jealousy on her own part. She didn't do jealousy. Although maybe if she'd exhibited a little, she might not have found her fiancé in bed with her room-mate. It was hard to let herself off the hook for her naiveté.

Her roommate and so-called friend previously insisted she didn't think much of Dalton, Maddie's ex, which might have been true, but it didn't stop her jumping into bed with him at their first opportunity. Maddie had been away for a weekend, which had apparently left the door open for a quick fling. Unfortunately, she'd come home early to show off her trophy to find the bedroom door literally *was* left open.

Some things, you couldn't unsee.

The mayor banged a gavel, and the crowd went quiet. At least, most of them did.

Denise pulled out a small card. "The winner of the Best Pie is...Maddie Flynn! I tried it myself and concur it was the best one today, and in my humble opinion, the best apple pie I've ever tasted." She gave her stomach a pat. "And I've tasted a few."

There was a round of applause mixed with laughter. Maybe not as loud as it might have been, since the Blue Brigade—a name that seemed to be stuck in Maddie's mind, so she'd have to watch herself at the bakery—were still annoyed. She hoped all that ill will wouldn't affect her sales next week.

She wouldn't enter the contest again. It wasn't worth the hassle.

"Congratulations." Denise climbed down from the temporary stage to hug her. "Well deserved. It's even better than I remembered."

"You remember my pie?"

Denise was a good friend now, but because she was a little older than Maddie, they hadn't run in the same circle for a good part of their school years.

Maddie noted a slight sheen to Denise's face, and she was paler now. Maybe all the tasting she'd done was too much for her?

"How could I forget the smell of your Gran's kitchen and the taste of that particular pie?" Denise asked.

Maddie laughed. "How silly of me. I forgot, not only is Gran a great cook, she loved to feed all the kids in the neighborhood."

"She did, and whether she particularly liked them or not didn't matter one bit. And you're cut from the same cloth. I hear you'll be contributing to feed the homeless and needy."

Maddie flushed. Having those words come from a friend meant a great deal, but she didn't expect accolades for doing what was right.

"Can we keep that between us?" she asked.

"You and Ethan make a good pair. You both hate to be in the limelight."

Maddie fidgeted, not comfortable with everyone pushing her and Ethan together, even in a sentence. "What do you say to having a drink together?"

"Tea?" Denise pointed outside to another tent where tables and chairs had been set out.

"Are you kidding me? I need something stronger, after the week I've had," Maddie scoffed.

Denise looked at her watch. "It's three in the afternoon."

"Yes, but it's five o'clock somewhere, isn't it?"

Denise threw an arm around her shoulders. "Oh, I've missed you. We haven't had nearly as many fun things going on since you left. I'll go find Laura and see if she wants to come—we were going to walk home together. You don't mind, do you?"

It was on the tip of Maddie's tongue to say she actually did mind, but it really wasn't a big deal. After all, she didn't know for sure Laura was involved in badmouthing her, either now or in the past, and maybe it was time she tried harder to make friends with her.

"The more, the merrier. I'll wait by my car. It's several rows back, in the middle."

Denise waved as she made her way through the tent to find Laura, who'd disappeared not long after the winners were announced. Maddie noticed Laura had also entered an apple pie. Maybe, since she hadn't won anything, she was disappointed.

Maddie could see Suzy talking to Angel. Knowing Denise would find it hard to get away from her constituents, she headed their way.

"Congratulations! I told you you'd win." Angel tucked her arm through Maddie's and squeezed.

"Thanks. To celebrate, I'm going for a drink with Denise. You're all invited."

"Congratulations, Maddie. Tell me where you're headed, and I'll meet you once I'm sure my MC job is done," Suzy said.

"I'll be there as soon as I collect the cakes I bought."

Suzy rolled her eyes at Angel. "I'll come with Angel, because I'm sure she'll need more than two hands. This will be great. It's been forever since we all got together. Painting doesn't count."

Maddie grinned. "I know exactly what you mean. We're meeting at O'Malley's."

Looking forward to being with the Girlz, she began to weave her way through the tent and then the parking lot. She was glad to get to her Jeep; the trophy was heavy. Thank goodness she'd left the top down to keep Honey cool. She threw her bag onto the back seat and had one foot in the door when she saw something fluttering in the slight breeze. A colorful cloth was wrapped around her back tire.

She went to pull it off and saw it was a scarf. It looked like one of Angel's. She pulled it gently at first so as not to tear it, then pulled harder, but it was stuck fast. Thinking to try another angle, she moved around the back.

Her hand shot to her mouth, and she fell to her knees.

A body was lying behind the wheel.

Denise's body. One sensible shoe lay sadly on its side by her foot.

Maddie had heard when you saw something like this, you lost the ability to scream, and that seemed to be true in her case.

She reached for her friend's wrist with a shaking hand. No pulse. Denise's lips were blue, and there were specks of blood around her mouth. Her fair hair had made a halo around her head, and her eyes were staring blankly back at Maddie.

Dear Lord, Denise looked dead!

Chapter Thirteen

Maddie was no medic, but it didn't look like Denise had simply fainted. Panic clawed at her, pulling her into an abyss that seemed to have no end—until she saw Ethan. Being so tall, he was easily visible behind the cars, and was the perfect person to help her. Fortunately, he was walking her way.

No! He veered off toward his own car, which she'd happened to notice earlier was a few rows away to the right.

"Help!" Her voice was nothing but a squeak.

He was farther away now, but the fear of being left alone with Denise and having no idea how to help her gave Maddie the ability to scream.

"HELP! Ethan!"

He stopped and looked around, searching for her. She waved madly, and, to her intense relief, he came running.

"Maddie? Are you okay?" he called.

She shook her head and pointed behind her.

"What is it?" He was level with her car.

"Not what. Who."

Ethan walked around the back and hissed through his

teeth. "Denise." He bent down and tossed Maddie his phone. "Looks like a heart attack. Call the paramedics!"

He dropped to his knees and took Denise's pulse, then leaned down to her lips. Maddie had already done both of those things, and no amount of wishful thinking would make a difference, but she was glad for the second opinion, because Denise wasn't breathing. Looked around, he spied the scarf and ripped it from the wheel with a horrible tearing sound. After wiping Denise's mouth with one corner, he began CPR.

Thankful he knew what to do, Maddie moved away to make the call. It was difficult to speak when the tears were falling down her cheeks and into her mouth. The emergency number rang two or three times, then she was hit with a barrage of questions.

She had questions of her own, but they would have to wait.

Finally, a siren sounded in the distance, but it seemed like forever before the paramedics joined them. The two men took over treating Denise, which allowed Ethan time to catch his breath. He came over to Maddie and took back his phone.

"I'll call this in, then you can tell me what you know."

Maddie moved to the front of her car, away from the scene, not wanting to know what the paramedics were doing but feeling it was all too late. *Was it true, could Denise really be dead?*

Denise had been one of the mean girls back in the day, Maddie remembered: a friend of Virginia and her group. Being part of that group meant there was no reason for Denise to mix with the nerdy girls like Maddie and her friends, although all of them had been jealous of Angel back then and made her life hell.

Suzy, Angel, and Maddie had started high school in Destiny two years after Virginia's group and had attempted to stay out of their way by keeping a low profile, which was always going to be hard for Angel, especially when the high school jock took a shine to her, much to the annoyance of the mean girls.

It was like that for the whole year, and then something happened. Denise had a major argument with Virginia—no one knew exactly what it was about—and she was ostracized. It meant she spent a lot of time on her own, since everyone else was wary of getting in the middle of anything that involved Virginia.

The up side was Denise's grades improved. Majorly.

It was Angel, upset that anyone was left on their own, who'd suggested they extend an invitation for Denise to join them one lunchtime. To everyone's surprise, Denise jumped at the offer. She apologized many times for her behavior and thanked them for giving her a chance.

From that first lunch on, she'd been a nicer, happier person. She'd won their hearts and, in time, the hearts and respect of the whole town, through her selfless behavior, doing what she could for anyone in need. She'd also won the mayoralty by a landslide.

Tears welled up in Maddie's eyes. This couldn't be the end for Denise.

Several people were walking to their cars trying to rubberneck when they saw the paramedics. Ethan headed them off.

"We've had an incident, folks. Please stay back until my deputies get here and we've checked over the surrounding area. We'll advise you when it's okay to leave."

Ethan was good at his job. His voice commanded even the overly curious, and they came no farther.

Maddie started to shiver, which turned into some all-out shaking. *Darn it.* She didn't want to go to pieces.

Although it seemed much longer, it was only a minute or two before a pair of sheriff's department cars pulled into the parking lot. Ethan waved them over, and they came as close as they could to Maddie's car before the deputies riding in them jumped out.

Maddie couldn't avoid hearing the conversation. Denise was pronounced dead, and a deputy began to take pictures. A lot of pictures.

Ethan put his arm around her shoulders. "Maddie, come sit in the car. This has been a heck of a shock."

Gratefully she agreed, since standing was becoming difficult. Eventually, a paramedic covered the mayor with a sheet, which Maddie could see playing out in her rearview mirror.

One of the deputies and Ethan came around to her. "How are you holding up?" Ethan asked.

"I'm okay."

"No, you're not. You're shaking like a leaf. The food tent is just over there. I'm sure we can find a quiet corner where we can talk. I'm going to try to find one of the Girlz to sit with you."

She nodded, allowing herself to be led there, where she slumped into a chair.

Ethan and the deputy sat beside her. "Take your time and tell us what you know," Ethan said.

Maddie bit her lip, then took in a deep breath. "Nothing. Absolutely nothing. I went back to my car, and I was about to get in when I saw something under my back wheel fluttering in the breeze. When I went to check, there she was. Already dead," she finished in a rush.

The deputy had a pad out. "I understand the mayor was a friend of yours?"

Maddie lifted her chin. "She *is* a friend of mine."

Ethan blanched a little, then took over the questioning. "Of course. The mayor's car doesn't appear to be on site. Do you know why she was in the parking lot by your car?"

"Yes. We were going out for a drink. I was going to drive them."

"Them? Was there someone else other than the two of you involved?"

Maddie's mind sifted through his words. "Laura. What do you mean by 'involved'?"

Ethan ignored that. "So, it was the three of you meeting up?"

"Yes. No. Suzy and Angel were coming too. A little later."

Ethan gave their full names to the deputy, who was scribbling frantically, then said, "Where were you headed?"

"To the bar in town."

"O'Malley's?"

Her head was throbbing. "Yes. Was it a heart attack?"

The crowd had noticeably thinned, and she guessed most of them would have heard the gruesome story by now. Maude Oliver and a few of the Blue Brigade from the Country Club stopped near their table to stare. Ethan ignored them while Maddie tapped her fingers on her thighs and closed her eyes for a moment.

"Rob, can you move these people along?"

The deputy did as he was asked, and Ethan leaned toward Maddie. "I shouldn't say anything, and I can't be certain, but thanks to the course I was just on, I noticed a distinctive smell around Denise's mouth," he said quietly. "I think she was poisoned, and I'm pretty sure it was arsenic."

Maddie gasped. "Poisoned? But how?"

Her exclamation had him looking around again for eavesdroppers. "She tasted quite a few cakes and pies today. It could have been any of them, or maybe it was something else."

"That would explain why she looked the way she did," Maddie whispered.

Ethan's concern turned to suspicion. "What do you mean? Did you see something?"

"When I went to invite her to come for a drink, she was sweaty and pale. I thought it was because she'd overdone things. You know how much she gives of her time to the community and . . ."

"Sweaty and pale? I see." Ethan pulled out his own notebook and scribbled a few lines.

Maddie had a thought that wouldn't stay inside her head. "You don't seriously think it was food poisoning, do you? I can't bear to think it had anything to do with my pie, or anyone else's."

Ethan looked up apologetically, as if the thought had never occurred to him, which gave her a small amount of relief. "It *might* be food poisoning, and if it is I'm sure it had nothing to do with you."

"If it was, then somebody did this on purpose?" she pressed.

"I didn't say that."

He had insinuated it, though. "Whatever happened you need to find out who is responsible as soon as possible. Don't waste your time with me." The words caught in her throat. With so many people in town for the festival, they needed to start the search right away.

"This is all part of that. You could have been the last person to see her and sometimes we know things which we might not remember right away."

"Sorry. Please hurry. I need to go home. I feel... dirty." The last word came out as a croak.

Ethan nodded. "It's natural, and I hear that a lot. This won't take much longer."

The deputy came back not long after. "Everything's clear outside, Sheriff."

"Good man. Did you find Ms. Flynn's friends?"

"No. One of them was taken in for questioning. The others are being processed with the crowd."

"Okay. Get someone to talk to the people on this list, and we'll need to track down all the stallholders." He turned back to Maddie. "I'll take you home to freshen up, then, when you feel up to it, we need to head over to the station so you can give a statement."

"I can't leave my car."

He looked at her like she was crazy. "You're not driving in this state. Plus, we have no idea what this is about or who's involved. I'll get one of the deputies to follow us in your car, if it makes you feel better."

Honey had been tucked up in Gran's garage since Maddie moved to New York City, and was a major plus in coming home. It was a knee-jerk reaction to make sure she came to no harm. Still, leaving her in the deputy's care didn't compare with what had happened to Denise.

Maddie felt unconnected to this reality and didn't have the strength to explain. Not only was Denise dead, but a killer might be walking around among them. Things like that didn't happen in Maple Falls.

She let Ethan take her arm again and lead her to his car. He opened the passenger door, and as she slid onto the leather seat he issued orders to his team, who had followed them. He spoke quickly and firmly about them talking to as many people as possible and tracking Denise's whereabouts through the afternoon.

Maddie shivered again. Her thoughts were all over the place, and she didn't hear Ethan until he put his hand in front of her face, palm up. "They'll need the keys."

"Sorry?"

"Keys? For your car."

His voice had that patient tone usually reserved for children or the elderly. She swallowed hard, feeling like a mixed bag of both.

"My keys are in my purse, which is in my car. I threw it on the back seat. The top's down."

He didn't fuss over her burbling and waited patiently until his deputy returned with her purse. Giving the man her address, he made sure she was buckled up, then they were on their way.

The day was still sunny, but she was cold and felt as if a gray cloud full of rain was hanging over her. Something terrible had happened, but the rest of the town looked the same. Nothing had changed, except Denise was gone.

When the shaking began again in earnest, she was extremely glad Ethan was driving.

How could this be real?

Chapter Fourteen

On the drive home, they were both so quiet it was almost painful, but for the life of her, Maddie couldn't think what to say. She knew nothing, had seen nothing, but she might have been the last one to talk to Denise. The last...apart from the killer. How had this happened in a sweet town like Maple Falls? Nothing about this made sense.

Ethan parked behind the shop and helped her out of the car as if she were an invalid. That wouldn't do. She had responsibilities and needed to call Gran who would be devastated. She straightened her back and went to the mat at the back door to pick up her spare key albeit with a shaking hand. After several stubborn attempts to get it in the keyhole, he held his hand out, and she conceded he'd probably manage to open it a lot faster.

As he did, the deputy arrived behind them in Honey. The younger man trotted up the path and handed Ethan her keys, then ran back to a waiting patrol car.

"Thank you!" she called after him, her voice deep with emotion as Ethan gestured for her to proceed him.

Once inside, she climbed the steps up to her apartment and sank onto a chair while Ethan went straight to the kettle in the small kitchen. "Tea or coffee?"

She licked her dry lips. "Tea, please. I guess a drink is out of the question if I have to go to the station."

He paused. "Not necessarily. Will it help?"

Maddie put her face in her hands. "Probably not," she mumbled.

"Tea it is, then."

"I better ring Gran and tell her. I hope the Girlz are okay," she muttered to his back.

Picking up her phone she saw a list of missed calls and messages. She listened to Gran's first. It was hard to hear the sad voice, full of concern, but a relief to hear the Girlz were taking care of her. They had called, then come to the Bakery, and would stay with Gran until Maddie got there. She sent a message back to say she was fine and would be at the station for a while, and not to worry. Now, she could focus on what needed to be done. Then she could be with her family.

A warmth around her ankles could only be Big Red, and when he jumped onto her lap and made soft noises against her neck, she buried her face in his fur, willing herself not to cry.

A couple of minutes later, she felt Ethan's hand on her shoulder. "Here you go. I added plenty of milk."

Big Red took a sniff at the milky concoction, which was just the way she liked it, then moved back so she could take a sip. She was surprised Ethan remembered how she took her tea. Then again, he was dealing with a stressed witness, so it was more than likely he didn't want her to scald her mouth.

Ethan walked around the open-plan apartment. "I like

what you've done with the place. I never came upstairs, but I heard it was a shambles."

A change of subject was welcome. "It was really awful. There were holes in the floor, and everything was dated and dreary when I moved in, just like downstairs. I like color."

"You always did. Color suits you."

She felt her cheeks heat despite the matter-of-fact way he'd said it. "Thank you."

He nodded. "How's the shop doing?"

"I thought it would slow down after that crazy first day, but it's getting busier. I desperately need help. Hindsight is a marvelous thing; you know? I should have had that organized before I opened. I was too impatient, wanting to start paying back my loan as soon as possible. I needed at least another week to get things sorted properly." She was babbling and didn't know how to stop.

"It's good the business is doing well, and I'm sure you'll get a taker for the job soon. Most people in town respected Denise, but did she ever say to you or the Girlz that she might have any enemies?"

She raised an eyebrow at his deliberate maneuver. "You're good at this sheriff thing, aren't you?"

He shot her a quick grin. Ethan had very nice white teeth, she noticed. Perfectly straight. Those braces he'd hated so much had clearly done their job.

"I've had some practice," he said. "Enemies? Did she have any?"

"Of course. Who doesn't?"

"I don't think I have," he said wryly.

"Really? Haven't you put people in jail? Given evidence that a criminal held a grudge about?"

His lips fought a smile. "Hmm. You seem to be feeling better. Now, back to Denise."

"Don't forget I've been mainly out of town for years." When he merely waited for more, Maddie sighed. "There are bound to be disagreements. Denise was in local government after all. But I haven't heard about anyone or anything lately she was upset about. People around here seem to get along pretty well, for the most part."

He nodded encouragingly.

She swallowed hard. "I can give you a list of the mean girls she associated with when we were at school, but Denise didn't have anything to do with them anymore. You would have known them. Anyway, most of them don't live here, they left as soon as they could, looking for bright lights and more fun than Maple Falls could provide."

Tapping the pen against his chin, he thought for a minute. Then he asked quietly, "Like you?"

She was shocked. Where had that come from? "Me leaving was totally different. I had a plan to be a great business woman, not be seen in all the right places."

"A famous business woman?"

"Not necessarily. Being great at something doesn't mean you have a craving for being famous."

"I would have thought they were synonymous."

She was growing more irritated by the moment. "Not for me. I wanted to come home knowing I was good at something I'm passionate about. It was, it is, enough."

"But you hadn't intended on coming home just yet. And, knowing you are an excellent baker, why did you enter the contest?"

She squeezed Big Red a little harder, and he let out a warning growl but stayed on her lap. "I'm happy to be home, regardless of the circumstances. As for the contest, that was a mistake. I don't know why I thought it was a good idea. For Denise's sake, I wish I hadn't."

"Why? Do you think her death is somehow connected to the competition?"

Maddie threw her hands in the air, which juggled the cat enough to make him growl again. "I don't know. Maybe if I hadn't been there, if I hadn't suggested going to O'Malley's for a drink, she might not have been in the parking lot right at that moment. The killer might not have had the opportunity to hurt her."

Ethan shook his head. "As true as that might be, if the person wanted Denise to be their victim, a determined killer would find a way and not be deterred by circumstances."

She gulped. "That doesn't make me feel any better."

"Sorry. How *do* you feel?"

"The shaking's not so bad. I don't feel sick anymore."

"Good news if you're riding in my car," he said straight-faced.

Any other time, she would have laughed. "I could go in mine."

"I don't think you should drive just yet. Let me take you, then I'll bring you home so you can have that drink."

Maddie licked her lips. As nice as the tea had been, the thought of having a sip or two of something stronger was certainly appealing. Purely for medicinal reasons, since this nightmare was still feeling surreal, despite her having been an eyewitness. She couldn't believe she would never see Denise again, or that she and Ethan were calmly talking about who would want to kill her.

"Give me a minute."

She bolted to her bedroom and stared at her stricken face in the mirror. She wasn't the same person who had left here this morning, and she doubted she would ever be again.

With a trembling hand, she brushed her tangled hair then went to the bathroom to wash her face and hands which made her feel marginally better. A few minutes later, she and Ethan were on their way to the station.

When they arrived, Laura was ahead of them, about to enter another room with a deputy. She turned a tear-stained face toward Maddie, and their eyes met. Laura's lips trembled, and Maddie took a step towards her, knowing how she must be feeling, but the Deputy pushed Laura gently inside and shut the door.

Another half-dozen people lined the hall, all people from the fair, all of them looking a little dazed. The murder, Maddie realized, wasn't going to affect only her group of friends. The whole town would have their belief that they were safe in this little corner of the world shattered.

Ethan led her to a room opposite the one Laura was in, where another deputy waited. A small machine was sitting in the center of a nearby table. Maddie's mouth went dryer than a leaf in fall at the idea of being recorded. She didn't know what she should say or what she might know that would help.

There was also a cloud of guilt over not being able to save Denise, and the guilty feeling anyone would get when talking to the law, as if she had in fact done something wrong.

She sat in the metal chair and nervously waited for them to begin.

"Deputy Jacobs will be conducting this interview," Ethan said.

Maddie nodded, and Ethan smiled encouragingly. The other man didn't smile, and he began the interview.

"Tell me everything you know about what the mayor was doing prior to her death."

Maddie explained about the pie competition and winning the top prize. "My friends and I were going to meet Denise at O'Malley's. I thought I was leaving before her," she finished with a wobble.

"Whose scarf was it we found at the scene?"

"Scarf? Oh, you mean the one I saw wrapped around my tire as I was getting into my car?"

"Yes."

"I have no..." Then Maddie remembered seeing it around someone's neck earlier that day. "I believe it might be Angel's. She wears one like that. Actually, anything bright."

"I see."

She didn't like the sound of that. "But Angel wouldn't have had anything to do with Denise's death. We were all friends."

The deputy raised an eyebrow.

Anger bubbled inside her. "No, really. You should put your time into finding the killer, not questioning Denise's friends."

Ethan gave her a sympathetic look. "It's his job."

"Well, I don't happen to like the way he's doing it."

"Ms. Flynn," the deputy continued, "we don't know for sure that this was a murder, but we are treating it as suspicious. You've said more of your friends were planning to meet up. Can you confirm they are Angeline Broome, Suzy Barnes, and Laura McKenzie?"

She folded her arms and nodded, but refused to entertain the idea that her friends were potential suspects, even though she had little to add about anyone's whereabouts.

There followed more questions that Maddie couldn't answer and she had the distinct impression the deputy thought she wasn't co-operating.

"I think that's all for now, Ms. Flynn," the deputy said tersely as he rose, turned off the machine and left the room.

Maddie glared at Ethan, who shrugged unapologetically. "Nobody's being accused of anything, but there are rules and guidelines which need to be followed in any investigation. Often, something you never dreamed of could turn out to be a vital clue."

"It wasn't Angel," she said stubbornly.

"I agree."

Sagging into her chair with relief, she let out a hitching breath. "Why?"

"For one thing, Angel didn't leave the cake tent for most of the morning, which would have been her main opportunity. She was always surrounded by people which would have made it hard to add anything to a cake or pie."

She knew he was trying to ease her fears, but it wasn't working. How awful would it be if they accused Angel because of something she'd said? If there was anyone from their group who might be involved, it was more likely to be Laura.

She bit her lip, feeling suddenly guilty over her thoughts. Should she tell Ethan anyway? Her head hurt, thinking about it.

She pointed to the door. "I see they're talking to Laura."

Ethan pulled his chair closer. "They are. Maddie, if you know something you need to tell me no matter who it concerns."

She hesitated. "It may be nothing, and I don't feel good about saying this."

"It won't go any further than this room if I can help it."

"Laura might have some problems with jealousy." Maddie blurted, already feeling ashamed.

"Yes?" he said encouragingly.

"That's it."

"Who was she jealous of? Denise?"

"Maybe."

"Maddie?"

She clasped her hands tightly on the table. "All right. It's me. I was Angel's best friend, and then Laura latched on to her while I was in New York City. When I would visit she avoided me, then when I came back to stay, she didn't seem very happy about it. She... She also baked a pie." The words left a sour taste in her mouth.

"Thanks. I'll check on her statement when I get yours. It's being printed for you to sign now, then you can go home."

True to his word, it wasn't too much longer before the paperwork arrived, and Ethan placed it in front of her.

"This is what you told the deputy. Please check that it's correct and sign at the bottom."

He was being professional, but she didn't like the change in his tone. Was he suggesting something was wrong with what she'd said, something she might like to change? She felt like she'd been pulled through a wringer. All she wanted to do was to get back home, but she took pains to read statement, before hastily scrawling her signature.

Ethan took her home, helped her out of his car, and walked her up the steps. He still had her keys, and after he'd opened the back door, he put them in her hand.

"Do you want me to come up?"

"I don't think that's necessary, but thanks." She didn't mean to sound ungrateful but she did need to talk to Gran and the family.

"I could check your apartment."

As nice as the offer might be, it didn't help with the

jitters she was experiencing. "Is there some reason I should be afraid?"

"I don't think so."

"Way to reassure a girl, Sheriff."

Ethan looked exasperated. "I don't want you to be scared. Just careful."

"What do you suggest?"

"Make sure you lock all the windows and doors, especially when you're home alone, and no leaving keys under mats."

His censure was light, but she knew she wouldn't do that again. Steeling herself for the answer to a question which had been bugging her, she blurted it out. "Do you think the killer is still in town?"

Ethan took a minute, as if he was weighing up what to say.

"Until we know what the cause of death is, we won't know if there even is a killer, if there is a motive, or what it could be."

She sighed, suddenly wanting the security his presence offered. But he had work to do. They needed to know why Denise had died, and if it was murder, then the killer must be found. That was the most important thing for Ethan to be doing, not babysitting her.

She lifted her chin. "Denise was a good person and well-respected in this town. If it was murder, it's too awful to contemplate that someone from Maple Falls would harm her."

"The motives of a killer often seem irrational or ridiculous to the rest of us. To them, they're very real issues. That's why we have to sort through any and all information we can find."

His little speech put a lot of what had happened into

perspective. "Do the town a favor and find the truth, Ethan."

Her voice was light, but she was feeling so emotional that when he squeezed her shoulders, she contemplated falling into his arms, remembering what a good hugger he was.

"I intend to. We'll talk soon."

Oblivious to her internal dilemma, he walked away, tall and strong, while Maddie felt like a lump of dough with all the air thumped out of it.

She should have gone straight to the cottage, but she needed a moment to compose herself.

Chapter Fifteen

To Maddie's surprise, Gran was in the apartment. She'd heard Maddie arrive with Ethan and was waiting at the top of the stairs with Big Red, her eyes filled with tears, and had no doubt heard every word. Maddie waited for her to come down and they hugged with Big Red walking between their legs. Then they sank onto the couch.

"I can't believe it." Gran said after a minute or two.

"It's crazy. I'm sorry I didn't answer my phone, it was on silent."

"You had a terrible shock. The Girlz came by as soon as the deputies let them leave the festival. When I insisted on being back here to wait for you, they brought me and waited a while. We did get your text, so I wasn't worried. I knew Ethan would look after you. Do you want to talk about it?"

Maddie nodded. She explained her version of events and Gran listened in horror.

"I wish I had been there with you."

"I'm glad you weren't. It was a very long day and you've been so ill. How are you feeling now?"

"Much better than this morning, but I am dog tired."

"Me too. Let's try and get some sleep."

They went up the stairs together. Exhausted Maddie struggled to change into her pajamas. Big Red, always sensitive to her moods snuggled up close to her, wrapping his long tail around her arm. He stayed there all through the long night, when sleep was fleeting.

Well before dawn and after hours of tossing and turning, she went downstairs to bake, even though it was Sunday.

Gran was already there, making a pot of soup. "I hope I didn't wake you, sweetheart."

"Not at all. I was lying there thinking about things until I couldn't stand it anymore."

"I know what you mean. Tea?"

Maddie nodded. "I'll make it."

Gran put the last of her soup ingredients into the pot, cleaned up, then joined Maddie at the counter to watch the sky lighten over the fields across the road. It was going to be a beautiful day, Maddie thought, but it seemed wrong to enjoy it.

"How are you feeling today? Has your stomach settled?"

Gran broke the silence. "I'm much better. Still a little queasy, but I'm thinking it's more about poor Denise. Do you really think she was poisoned?"

"I don't know, but from what Ethan said, it looks likely. We should keep that between us though."

Gran nodded. "Will we open tomorrow?"

"At first, I thought no, but at least it will keep us busy. What do you think?"

"I'll get some brownies and cookies made this afternoon."

"I'll make some pies." Then Maddie shuddered, reconsidering. "No, I won't make any pies for a couple of days. Cake would be better."

Gran pursed her lips. "You're probably right not to. Pies were the last thing she tasted, and no matter that we know it had nothing to do with us, some of Maple Falls residents will likely point fingers." She sighed. "I'll make us some breakfast, then I might go over to the cottage and do some more packing."

"I could come help."

"No, you've got enough to do here sweetheart, and someone needs to watch the soup. Maybe you could try to figure out that coffee machine everyone keeps talking about. Either that, or you should hide the darn thing."

Gran was trying to lighten the mood, but all Maddie could muster was a nod, relieved that Gran didn't want her to go to the cottage today.

A little while later, as Maddie was finishing the dishes and Gran was stirring her soup, Angel appeared at the back door. The moment she was inside, they were in each other's arms, crying like babies

"Isn't it awful?" Angel said when her tears slowed. "Poor Denise. Poor you. I wasn't sure whether to come over last night, but I figured the last thing you needed was more questions. I wanted to find you after the deputies let us leave the fair, but you were already at the station."

"How did you know?"

"Laura called and told me you were there the same time she was. I would have liked to be with her too, but she told me to stay with Gran and Suzy."

Maddie nodded. "Thanks for staying with Gran and I was pretty exhausted by the time I got home."

"I can't imagine how you must have felt. Laura was

devastated. She was at Denise's only that morning, and they'd walked to the fair together."

"Denise told me. I was going to drive us to O'Malley's, and they were meeting me at my car."

"That's right. It must have been such a shock to find her there."

"More than I can say. I was worse than useless. Thank goodness Ethan arrived and knew what to do, but we were too late."

"There was so much confusion. Deputies everywhere, trying to talk to as many people as they could, and people getting in the way. We were all upset, and we couldn't get to you." Angel let out a half-sob.

Maddie felt the tears begin again, even though she'd thought she couldn't possibly cry anymore.

"The deputies asked me about my scarf," Angel said. "I felt sick about it."

"Why was it there?" Maddie fetched a box of tissues and handed it to Angel after taking a handful for herself.

"Denise wasn't feeling so good, so I dampened the scarf, and she had it around her neck to keep her cooler."

At that moment, Suzy burst through the door with Laura behind her. They saw Angel's and Maddie's misery, and the four of them turned into a sobbing mess.

Gran crossed the kitchen and ushered them to the stools at the counter. "You Girlz sit down. We'll have a nice cup of tea and a slice of this cake Maddie's just baked."

"That would be wonderful, Gran," Angel hiccuped.

Maddie was glad of this little touch of normality. "It's such a relief you don't think it was my pie that killed Denise."

Suzy gasped. "Don't be ridiculous. You wouldn't do

something like that. Is that what they think killed her? A pie?"

Maddie flushed, knowing Ethan hadn't wanted his suspicion of poison to be broadcast. But these were her friends. Surely, he wouldn't mind. "Please don't spread it around, because they still have to do an autopsy."

"We won't say a word. Go on," prompted Suzy. "We know you found Denise and that Ethan tried to revive her. Tell us what happened at the station and what they said."

"They sure made it sound like it was poisoning, and they were just waiting for confirmation. Denise has no record of heart disease that I know about, so I guess it was a fair assumption to make."

Angel nodded. "That's right. Denise had to have a full medical exam when she ran for mayor. Laura had one too, didn't you?"

"I did." Laura's face was puffy from crying, and she looked like she wasn't done yet.

Gran shook her head. "It's a stupid assumption, as far as I'm concerned. Not the poisoning, but that it could have been from any of the contest food at the fair."

"That's right. It could have been any number of things," Suzy agreed.

"You know, she'd been complaining about not feeling so great for a couple of days. I went over on Friday afternoon to see how she was. She seemed perkier, but that probably had more to do with her secret admirer, I would think." Gran had a small, sad smile and a faraway look on her face.

Stunned silence filled the room.

"What secret admirer?" Angel was the first to voice the question.

Gran's smile vanished, replaced by a look of dismay. No doubt, she was surprised at herself for revealing a secret when she was well known for keeping them. Gran was always sought out by anyone who wanted to unburden themselves, and it appeared Denise had been no exception.

"You can't leave us hanging, Gran," Suzy pressed.

"She told me not to say anything, but I guess it doesn't matter now." Gran's guilt gave way to her resignation.

Maddie threw her hands up. "I think it does matter. They could be the killer."

Gran became flustered. "Oh my. Do you think so? I never gave it a thought. Then again, I couldn't imagine anyone would want to kill our Denise."

"Except for Virginia. She was apoplectic when she lost the election," Laura added.

"How did you feel about it?" The words slipped out before Maddie had a chance to reel them in.

Angel was immediately defensive. "Laura and Denise were close, even though they ran against each other and Denise won. There's no way she'd hurt anybody, let alone kill them. She's a gentle person." She put her arm around Laura's shoulder while frowning at Maddie.

"I'm sure Maddie didn't mean anything. It was a generalization about motives, wasn't it?" Suzy looked pointedly at Maddie.

"I was only saying Laura might understand how Virginia felt, since they were all political rivals." That hadn't come out so well, either.

Angel was outraged. "You're comparing Laura with Virginia?"

"Virginia's in a league of her own," Suzy said firmly.

"Darn straight she is," Angel agreed.

Laura sat quietly, pale and miserable, sipping her tea.

"Sorry, Laura." Maddie couldn't bear to see her this way. It made her feel like she'd kicked a puppy. "I made a mess of that, it's just that my head is still all over the place. Forgive me."

Laura sighed. "It's okay. The deputies questioned me for hours. I made a pie too. Judging by the people waiting to be interviewed after me, anyone who made a pie or cake that Denise might have tasted is probably under suspicion."

"Well, I'm glad I didn't enter anything this year. We know it wasn't anything you two baked, so we can rest easy on that score too," Gran stated, as if to put a lid on the conversation—or at least on the way it was headed.

"So, will you open tomorrow?" Suzy asked Maddie.

"Gran and I were just discussing that. I think we should. But I'm wondering if it might be disrespectful."

Suzy shook her brown curls. "We're all going to work tomorrow. Why shouldn't you?"

Maddie grimaced. "It's a little different if she was poisoned by a pie, isn't it?"

Gran patted her hand. "But we don't know that for sure. And like I said, if she was, it definitely wasn't yours. Or Laura's."

Suzy smiled gently. "Let's talk about Denise, and not in a sad way. She wouldn't have wanted that. She was always trying to cheer people up. I want to hear more about her secret admirer."

Maddie was glad to move the conversation in another direction. "Yes, lets. Do you have any details, Gran?"

Gran shifted uneasily on her chair. "She really had no idea who it was, or so she said. Each day for the past week, a bakery box came to her house with something sweet inside and a wee note to say he admired her and hoped to meet up very soon, but he was shy and wanted to be sure she was ready to date."

"Anything else?" Maddie pressed.

"The note also said she should be patient because all would be revealed and she would be surprised."

Angel shivered. "Does anyone else think that sounds creepy?"

Suzy shrugged. "It's because we know she was murdered. Or we think she was. If you got a note like that at any other time, you'd think it was romantic, or at least flattering."

"Would not," Angel said with fervor.

"To be fair, that's probably because you don't like men," Suzy teased.

"No, it's not. I like men fine. I just don't want one of my own right now. There's a difference."

Suzy and Angel arguing was another sign of normalcy. It meant absolutely nothing as far as their friendship was concerned, and it helped lighten the mood a little.

"Okay, but I'd be flattered," Suzy insisted.

Laura nodded. "As much as I hate to admit it, I think I would be too."

A knock at the kitchen door stalled the conversation. Ethan poked his head inside.

"Come on in. Would you like coffee?" Maddie stood and waved him to her seat.

He was in uniform, and he took off his hat as he entered. "I should have known I'd find you all together. Coffee would be great. How are we doing today?" he asked them all, but his eyes were on Maddie.

"We've been better," she answered, noticing that Laura was flushed and couldn't take her eyes off Ethan.

"I'm sure. Denise was my friend too, and this has hit everyone mighty hard." He turned to the group at the counter. "Since you're all here, maybe I could ask you ladies a few questions about yesterday?"

"Are we still under suspicion?" Suzy demanded.

Ethan put his hat on the counter and regarded them. "Not by me. But having said that—you might have facts you're not even aware of."

"What kind of facts?"

"Who was the last person to see her? How long had she been in the parking lot, and did anyone have a grudge against her?"

The women shared a look. Maddie caught Ethan's raised eyebrow and figured he'd notice something so obvious. He didn't say anything, but his look did have a great big question mark in it.

Maddie sighed. "Gran, tell Ethan about the boyfriend."

Gran spluttered and coughed. "That was shared in confidence," she said disapprovingly.

Ethan's seat was beside Gran's, so he patted her back and used his cajoling voice. "I'd be very interested in any information you have. It could be vitally important."

Apparently, the way he touched her gently on the shoulder and spoke as if she was the only one in the room was more than enough to get Gran to tell her story in far more detail than the Girlz had managed to pull out of her.

"Denise had an admirer who left treats on her doorstep."

A raised eyebrow was the only clue that he was surprised.

"How did she meet him?"

"She hadn't. Not yet. She was hoping to meet him face to face any day."

"So, some stranger was leaving her treats? Since when?"

"Only the past week."

"What kind of treats?" Ethan had his pad out and was writing furiously while Gran continued.

"A cupcake or two, in a bakery box."

He looked up. "What kind of box?"

"White, like ours. Nothing fancy. I thought at first he'd bought the cakes from here, because the boxes were exactly like ours including the logo. I assumed the company must have made more of them. Anyway, those cupcakes tasted nothing like Maddie's."

Everyone stared at her open-mouthed for the second time that morning, except for Ethan.

"You tasted them?"

"Just the once. Denise was trying to lose weight because of her admirer, so she was sharing them with anyone who stopped by. Only women, of course, because she didn't want to offend him if she really did know the man and he happened to turn up. Unfortunately, she hadn't been feeling so good last week, either, and she wanted me to take one from Friday home. I told her that giving cupcakes to a baker is like taking taffy to a candy store, so I said no. But I didn't want to be rude, so I tried a small piece. I have to say wherever the admirer got those cupcakes from, he needed to get his money back."

She looked around at the stunned group. "What's wrong with you Girlz? You look like you're swallowing flies."

Maddie took a deep breath. "Gran, you haven't been well."

Gran waved a hand in dismissal. "True, but I'm fine now."

Ethan shook his head. "When did you become unwell?"

Gran frowned. "Let me see. Thursday? Or was it Friday?"

"Friday," Maddie interjected.

"And when did you taste Denise's cake?" Ethan asked.

"Now, that was definitely Friday. I visited her to see how she was. About three o'clock. It was later that afternoon I felt queasy."

There was silence while they waited and watched as Gran came to the conclusion the rest of them had already reached.

Her hand went to her mouth. "That cupcake was poisoned? That's what killed Denise?"

"We can't be sure, but this is too much of a coincidence," Ethan replied. "And even more so if every cupcake that week was tainted. Now that we've got this information, I'll head over to Denise's house and see if I can find anything we might have missed yesterday. I'll get my deputies to talk to anyone who hasn't felt well this past week. Some of them may have been the recipients of Denise's generosity. Keep this conversation between us, and I'll catch up with each of you as soon as I can."

Maddie followed him to the door, where he turned. "It may be too late, but can you get Gran to have some tests this morning? I'll call Layla and ask her to open up for you." He looked at his watch. "In about an hour?"

"Of course. I'm sorry. I truly didn't know any of this."

He gave her a rueful grin. "Small towns can be a blessing and a curse when it comes to secrets. I'm just glad I know now."

She watched him go, thankful he had stopped by today and wondering if Gran had told him everything she knew. The Girlz stayed for a while longer, maybe hoping to find out more.

"I thought I knew her so well," Laura said.

"We all did." Angel squeezed her hand.

Maddie made another cup of tea for Gran and coffee for

the rest of them. "If only she had mentioned this secret admirer, we could have looked out for her."

Gran shook her head. "I don't think it would have helped. This person was obviously bent on anonymity."

"It makes me feel like we can't trust anyone," Suzy put in.

It was a sobering thought, one that made the hair on Maddie's arms prickle. "Drink up, Girlz. I have to get Gran down to the clinic for some tests."

"But I feel fine," Gran protested.

"Ethan wants Layla to see if there are any signs you might have the poison in your system, which would link it to the cupcakes."

"Oh."

Suzy got up. "We'll go, then. Let us know if you find out anything."

"I'm sure we'll have to wait a couple of days for the results," Maddie replied.

Angel hugged her. "Don't you worry about that. Ethan will push them through."

"I hope so. It'd be good to stop worrying about one thing."

"I hate the looks I'm getting." Laura bit her lip. "Everyone who baked is under suspicion."

"It'll be okay." Angel took her arm, and they walked out together.

Maddie wondered about the person who had initiated all this turmoil. And if it was one of their own...

She couldn't bear the thought. She needed to bake.

Chapter Sixteen

Ethan returned with his deputy on Sunday afternoon. A bakery box had been found in the mayor's trash. Since there were no other bakeries in town, Ethan apologetically took one of Maddie's boxes to the sheriff's department. It turned out to be a match, and there were traces of arsenic in it.

Once more, Maddie was at the sheriff's station being questioned by Deputy Jacobs, and this time they'd insisted Gran come in too. She was with another deputy in the room next door.

They'd better be taking care of her, Maddie thought.

"How do you think your bakery's box got to the mayor's house?" Deputy Jacobs began.

"Denise brought some things on the first day I opened. That was the only time she came in. According to Gran, Denise had an admirer who was leaving boxes for her."

Judging by his reaction, Jacobs knew about that. She looked to where Ethan was sitting in the corner. He gave her an apologetic look, but she had to accept this was evidence and she couldn't protect Denise from unkind thoughts anyone might have about her having an admirer.

"Boxes of cupcakes?" the deputy pressed.

"Yes."

"And you sold those cupcakes to this admirer?"

Maddie placed her hands on her thighs and her fingers began to tap. "I wouldn't know if I sold him any cupcakes, because I have no idea who this man is. What I do know is that the cupcakes in that box weren't mine."

He raised an eyebrow. "You know this how?"

"Gran said they were awful, and she should know how my food tastes."

"If they had poison in them, they might taste a little strange, wouldn't they?"

She was outraged. "I wouldn't poison my grandmother."

"But you'd poison the mayor, who the cupcakes were intended for?"

"You're twisting my words. I didn't poison anyone. Call the health department. They've already been in this morning and taken samples of everything, and your men searched my place and Gran's. Surely they'll give you the results if you ask." She folded her arms across her chest, remembering the sense of violation she'd felt.

Jacobs ignored her tirade. "Why would the mayor eat them if they tasted bad?"

"I have no idea. Maybe she didn't want to hurt her admirers' feelings or maybe she just tasted them, like Gran did."

"Your Grandmother is still alive."

"She only tried one cake. We don't know how many Denise tried, or finished, do we?"

The deputy gave that a moment. "How would someone get a bunch of your boxes if they didn't buy anything?"

Maddie was about to say she didn't know, when she had a sudden flash-back. "Maybe when my window got smashed it was on purpose and someone snuck in and helped themselves to the boxes."

Ethan gave her a surprised look but nodded in agreement. "Actually, Deputy, I was there after the window incident. The glass was all on the inside, meaning something broke it from the outside. The window is large enough for someone with a small build to get through."

Maddie frowned. "You were the one who said it must have been the wind."

Ethan ran his hand through his hair. "I was trying not to scare you, and I really didn't know for sure either way."

She was confused, and so was the deputy, who had turned slightly so he could see Ethan.

"Let me get this straight. There was a suspected break-in and you didn't report it?"

Ethan raised himself from the chair he'd been occupying. His six-foot-four body was noteworthy on an ordinary day. Right now, it was positively impressive as he glowered at his subordinate.

He spoke very slowly. "I didn't report it because I wasn't sure if it had been a break-in. I believed at the time that Ms. Flynn had found nothing missing. Therefore, there was no reason to think anything illegal had occurred."

The last thing Maddie wanted was to make Ethan look incompetent. She hadn't actually checked because she and Gran hadn't yet moved in any of their personal belongings, and she'd wanted to believe it was the wind.

"The thing is, Deputy," she said, "I wouldn't have had a clue if any boxes had been taken, because they were still in their packaging at that time. Once I started selling, I didn't keep track of how many I had in stock. It was a large order, sent to me as a present from a friend in New York City."

The deputy frowned at them both. "And you have no knowledge of the mayor's secret admirer?"

"None at all."

After several more questions in the same vein, Maddie was allowed to leave. She found her shell-shocked Gran already in the hallway.

Ethan followed Maddie out, and he gave Gran a worried look. "Take her home. I've got some tidying up to do around what happened in there, but I'll let you know if I hear anything."

She was about to do just that when another deputy handed Ethan a piece of paper. He held up a finger for them to wait while he read, then smiled.

"The report came back. Your place is clear."

Maddie shook her head. "That's good news, but it's a shame we didn't get it before we got dragged down here."

"I know, but we can't hurry the investigation. Go ahead and open the shop when you feel up to it."

"I think we'll leave it until after the funeral. Gran looks how I feel."

He nodded. "Try to get some rest, both of you, and please take care," he said earnestly, as he followed them out to the car.

When she had Gran settled and shut the door she turned to him and almost whispered, "Ethan, what did you mean, just then about taking care? Are we in danger?"

He ran his fingers through his hair and gave her a penetrating look, before glancing around them. Then he took her arm and pulled her a few feet away from the car. "Okay, I'm going to tell you something that you are not to share with anyone, and I should not be sharing with you."

He was also whispering, and she could hardly hear him from the pounding of her heart. She nodded, barely breathing.

"There was someone in the parking lot before you got there. With Denise. There was a scuffle. She had bruises on her wrists and throat. None of those things killed her—the poison definitely did that."

"Which means there really was someone walking around our town with the intention of killing her."

"Or maybe they miscalculated badly, and things went wrong. The point is they could still be around. Like I said before, I don't want you to be frightened, but please be careful. Make sure you lock up properly every night."

It was easy to say don't be frightened, but that didn't stop the thoughts running rampant through her head. Still, she must put on a brave face for Gran and it wouldn't hurt to practice. "I'll be fine. You don't need to worry about us when you've got a manhunt to take care of. Good luck."

"Thanks," he said, but she could see he was already thinking about what he needed to do.

Driving slowly, the drama of the last few hours making her head feel as though it was full of pudding, she'd never been happier to get out of a car.

"I wish we knew what was going on," Gran said.

"Me too. I don't like any of it, but I'm glad the shop has been cleared, and my pie."

"That's the only ray of light in all of this."

Maddie gave her a hug. This was more than a woman her age should have to deal with.

They drank several cups of tea, but their appetites were gone, so Gran went off to take a nap and Maddie called the Loughlins, Denise's parents, to say she could help out by catering the food for the funeral if they'd like her to.

They were lovely about it and made sure she understood that they knew Denise's death was no fault of hers, which was a huge relief.

Chapter Seventeen

O n Monday, a deputy called to say the results were back. Gran had minute traces of arsenic in her blood, but they shouldn't worry because her kidney function was almost normal. That was good news, but it meant Gran might have died had she eaten more of that cupcake. It could have been her and not Denise, and that was an awful road for the mind to be traveling down.

Maddie couldn't help fussing over Gran, who wanted none of that and was getting antsy at being made to feel like an invalid, but the tension wasn't confined to their apartment.

Reeling from Denise's death and the just-released knowledge it was officially classified as murder, the town went wild with gossip. Gran was informed via her friends from the community center of suggestions ranging from Denise having an affair with a prominent politician to being involved with a married man.

None of that sounded like the Denise she knew, and it made Maddie angry that people could be so tactless and disloyal. Of course, it wasn't everyone. People were naturally upset and wanted answers.

Every entrant in the competitions which had been judged by Denise was a suspect and treated warily, especially Maddie and Laura, until the sheriff's department ruled out all of them as suspects, since none of them had any poison in any of their pies, cakes or cookies on the day of the fair.

That was a major breakthrough, and it came as a relief, even if it only created more questions and suspicion. Maddie's bakery was closed all week out of respect, and considering several people had reported stomach upsets prior to the fair—which was the same week as her grand opening—she could understand if the townspeople had misgivings about returning when she reopened.

She also didn't feel she could donate her unsold baking until the matter was totally cleared up. It was all a mess, and she was exhausted from trying to come up with theories that might be the truth.

The funeral was the next day, and even though she had the all-clear, she was nervous about making food for the gathering afterwards. Denise's parents stood by their decision to include Maddie's baking, and for that she was grateful. She just hoped the few bad eggs who'd be attending wouldn't make a big deal of her food being there, which would upset the Loughlins.

Making dozens of cupcakes, brownies, sandwiches, and cookies, would be a bit much to do all in one day, so she'd make some of it tonight. It wasn't as if she could forget what had happened, so there was no relaxing going on, but baking had a way of making things clearer.

With that decision made, she decided to get some fresh air first. When she made a kissing sound, Big Red appeared by the door. He liked the evening walks she'd started after moving in, and he could do with the exercise since Gran was still feeding him tidbits when Maddie wasn't looking.

Together, they walked to the end of Plum Place, which ran along the back of all the stores to pick up her mail. They dawdled to smell the flowers along the edge of the road, and Big Red swatted a butterfly or two, but he saw no need to chase anything these days. She admired all the small gardens, so unusual at the backs of shops, which wouldn't be found anywhere except a small town like theirs.

The shop next to hers sold second hand appliances. Then there was the Angel's salon, and finally a butcher. Before the next block was the post office, where Maddie had a P.O. box. She'd thought that was a good idea, since Gran's house was going to be sold, but she often forgot to pick up her mail.

Maddie unlocked the small door of the box and pulled out her mail. There was a fair amount of it, most of which would be bills.

Big Red dawdled when they got back to the butcher's. It had caught his eye, or more likely his stomach, the day they moved back to Maple Falls, and he often wandered this way to see if the butcher had left out any treats for him.

Gruff Thomas Calder didn't tolerate animals, so it was a source of amusement that Big Red had formed this unlikely alliance.

"Come on, cat. The shops are all closed at this time of day."

Big Red sniffed and huffily followed her back to the bakery and into the kitchen. He jumped up onto an easy chair at the back of the room he'd decided was his while she flicked through the mail at the counter. She was right: it was mostly bills.

Apart from one envelope. It had her name and address typed on it by a real typewriter instead of being computer generated. She took it from the pile and caught the scent of perfume. Lifting it to her nose she sniffed. It was familiar, but not one she could name.

Her interest was piqued. She ripped the envelope open, and a single sheet of paper unfolded and fell to the floor. Maddie's heart skipped a beat as she retrieved it and smoothed it out on the table. In a classic whodunit way, the note was also typed.

If you know what's good for you, leave now!

Slumping onto a wooden chair, she reread the note. Who would have sent her such a thing, and why? What had she done, and how was she involved in whatever this was? It didn't make sense.

Gran chose that moment to come downstairs. "There you are. Any mail for me? I'm expecting—Maddie, what's wrong?"

She didn't have time to hide the letter before Gran plucked it from her shaking hands.

"Is this a joke?"

"I wish it was. It was in with the mail."

"I wonder what it means. Leave the shop, or Maple Falls in general?" Gran twisted her apron looking upset.

"The letter could have been posted yesterday, or days ago. I haven't bothered checking the mail this week."

Gran slapped her hand on the table. "Well, I think this is the work of a coward out to frighten you."

"Even so, I think I'll give Ethan a call. It must have something to do with Denise."

"Good idea. It doesn't hurt to have a big, strong man around the place."

Maddie turned to face her. "You're not scared, are you, Gran? I can take care of us."

"Of course you can, sweetheart. I'm just saying that Ethan, looking the way he does, could frighten any murderer away just by being here."

Maddie shivered. "Please don't use that word."

Gran took one of Maddie's hands in hers. "It isn't like you to be so jittery over anything."

"That was before I found Denise, and before I got the note. Now, I'm not sure who to trust."

"Most of the people in town know you, and they wouldn't do anything to hurt you. The police have ruled out your pie, and Denise wouldn't like you to feel guilty about not saving her, if that's what concerns you most."

Gran was right, but it was hard for Maddie to get her mind to accept she couldn't have done more. Since the murder, she hadn't slept for more than an hour or two at a time. Her go-to thought was, if only she had got to her car earlier. She might not have been able to capture the killer, but she might have been able to prevent Denise's death. She knew it was a what-if that couldn't change anything, but the mind could be a trap when an idea wormed its way in there. In real life as well as in your dreams.

"It's true and in my head I know it, but my heart is struggling to accept it. I should give Ethan a call and let him know about the letter."

"You do that, sweetheart, and I'll start on dinner."

The phone went to voicemail, and Maddie left a message for him to call her. She'd try again soon if she didn't hear back, but right now she needed to bake. It might not fix anything, but it sure made her feel better.

With relish, she pounded the dough while Gran cooked.

The easy silence and the physical work soothed her more than a stiff drink ever could. She was setting the dough aside to rest when the bell rang, and footsteps sounded in the shop. Startled, she managed to knock over the container of flour, and a cloud rose up over her. She'd forgotten to lock up, and that was a stupid thing to do right now.

Maddie picked up the rolling pin and crept to the curtain that separated the two rooms, motioning for Gran to stay where she was. Instead, Gran picked up a large knife and stood her ground, which didn't make Maddie feel even slightly safer.

"Maddie?"

She squealed and dropped her weapon of choice on her toes. Thank goodness she was wearing shoes, but it still hurt.

"What's going on?" Ethan burst through the curtain, from the shop.

Running straight into her, he knocked her flat on her back, landing on top of her. The air was forced from her lungs even as he put his arms out to catch most of his weight. He looked down at her with shock, his blue eyes so wide she could see several flecks of green in them. Had they always been there?

A movement caught her eye, and there was Gran standing over them, her hand at her mouth, her eyes crinkled with laughter.

"Gran," she warned.

"I see you two have everything under control, so I'll go about my business. Nice to see you, Ethan." With a noticeable spring in her step, she turned and went up the stairs, her shoulders shaking with laughter.

This was awkward.

"Ethan? Could you get off me?"

His eyes went wide, as if he hadn't realized where he was.

"Sorry. I heard you cry out and thought you were hurt." He climbed off and hoisted her to her feet.

"I was. Just not as bad as now." She rubbed her ribs.

"I'm sorry. I had no idea you were there, and when you yelled out, I really thought you were in trouble."

She gave him a doubtful look. "That's sweet of you. But I heard the bell, and since I'm not open, I thought you were an intruder."

"I could very well have been. I wasn't happy when I tried the door and found it unlocked. You need to be more careful right now. We did talk about that."

She didn't like being reprimanded, but he was right. "It was a silly mistake, and one I won't be repeating. To be honest, I've been all over the place since the murder. I was outside cleaning the window this morning, and I must have forgotten to lock the door."

His face softened, and it seemed like the right time to tell him about the latest development.

"I tried to call you earlier." She pulled the note and the envelope from her apron pocket. "I got this today."

He took it from her, and as he read, his other fist clenched. "This is serious. Someone is watching you, and we should probably assume it's someone involved in the murder."

Maddie grimaced. "I was trying not to go there."

Ethan laid the paper and the envelope on the table. "When did you get this?"

"It was in our box at the post office when I went to clear it earlier."

He took a plastic bag from his inside jacket pocket and placed the note and the envelope carefully inside. "We'll check them for fingerprints," he said in answer to her curious look.

"But why am I being targeted? I don't understand what anyone would have against me."

He gave her a skeptical look. "I'm sure you can think of one or two reasons."

"You can't mean the pie competition?"

"If jealousy was a motive, then I'd say definitely. Then there's the fact you were first on the scene. Perhaps the murderer imagines you saw them arguing. But let's not get ahead of ourselves. I'm glad you're doing okay. I appreciate you must be scared, and I want you to call me anytime if something else happens, no matter how small or seemingly insignificant it is. Or if you think of something that may help."

She nodded, feeling her stomach twist at the knowledge someone might be out to harm her. Potentially someone she knew.

"I'd better get going," Ethan said. "Please remember to lock up."

"I will."

They walked through the shop, and he stopped for a minute at the door, looking like he wanted to say something else. Instead, he nodded and waited outside until she had locked the door.

Having Ethan concerned about her was nice. Having a murderer watching her, not so much.

Chapter Eighteen

M addie had been up since dawn preparing the food. She wanted it to be special. Denise's parents had offered to pay her, but guilt aside, this was the last thing she could do for her friend, and she thought of it as a privilege, not a job.

The cupcakes, brownies, small sandwiches, and other items were all ready to go, and she was putting the final touches on the mini chocolate croissants, Denise's favorites.

The wake was to be at the town hall, which the family had set up to receive the anticipated large number of mourners. People stopped by and carried Maddie's wrapped goodies to the hall on their way to the church. Suzy, Laura, and Angel had done a wonderful job organizing this via the phone tree which was run through the school. It was touching how many people wanted to be involved. It gave everything a personal feel and restored a bit of faith into the community.

After Maddie and Gran dropped off the last few plates, they followed the procession to the church, which packed. People had to stand in the doorway, but the Girlz had saved Maddie a seat. Gran's group from the community center had saved her one near the front.

The Girlz held hands as the minister began the service. Denise's parents cried quietly in the front row, with close friends and family around them. It was as nice a service as it could be. Flowers adorned the church and the coffin, but nothing could take away from the somber mood.

Maddie had been asked to say a few words. It had been hard to think of something which wouldn't make her cry like a baby yet still convey how much Denise had meant, not only to her but to the town in general.

"Denise was a special lady who touched the lives of so many. She was a can-do person who sought to break down the barriers in our community with a cup of coffee and a chat. Denise was the sort of person you aspire to be like. She was approachable, kind, resourceful, clever, and inspirational. Outside of the mayor's job, at which she was a natural, Denise would help anyone, friend or not, who was in need, or simply be there to listen to a problem. She was always available."

Maddie looked out at the sea of faces, many sad and some thoughtful. "I think she would have been the mayor forever if it had been possible. Not because she would have wanted to, but because we wouldn't have let her quit."

That drew a smattering of laughter, and the Girlz smiled their encouragement.

"I'm convinced Denise has gone to a better place, because that's what she deserves. Just as I'm sure she knows how much we love and will miss her."

As Maddie moved back to her seat, she had to bite her lip to keep from crying. That had been the hardest thing she'd ever done. The Girlz hugged her, then resumed holding her hands.

The only thing that would make this more bearable would be if they found the killer, but she was glad no one had mentioned that today.

As they walked out into the beautiful sunshine, Maddie could see Ethan talking to Denise's parents. Out of uniform and wearing a dark suit, he was nodding at something Denise's father had said. The three of them looked so tired. Ethan had probably worked late last night, like she had, and Maddie hoped he'd made some progress. Denise's parents needed the closure, as did they all.

The Girlz were chatting with people wanting to offer condolences, but all Maddie could hear was buzzing as she gazed around. There seemed to be an awful lot of strangers here today. Her mind ran riot, wondering who they were and why they were here. Was the killer among them?

Seemingly out of thin air, a small, slender man in a crumpled suit bobbed up in front of her. He brushed past their group, knocking Maddie into her friends. Suzy was forced to take a step back.

"Rude," she muttered.

"Some people," Maddie agreed as her skin prickled. She wasn't a person who suffered from claustrophobia, but she imagined how she was feeling was something like it. Her skin was clammy, and her breathing was way too fast.

She was done with the crowd surrounding her, and it was getting hard to keep everything together. Could she leave? Only the family was headed to the crematorium for a final goodbye, so surely no one would think her uncaring.

"Let's pay our respects, then head to the town hall," she said. "I want to make sure the hot food has been heated and that there's enough tea and coffee." It wasn't a total lie; she really did care that everything was going to go smoothly.

"There's certainly enough food," Angel said. "The

tables were groaning when I dropped my plates off. You must have been up all night."

"Not all night, and Gran helped. Anyway, I've been having trouble sleeping, so it was good to have something to do."

Angel shook her head in exasperation. "I know how you feel. I've been tossing and turning myself, but you should have let us help, Maddie."

"You're so stubborn with the whole independence thing," Suzy added.

It was hard for Maddie to explain that she was worried about them being with her all the time without telling them about the note. She hated keeping secrets, but she couldn't bear to lose any of them. It was bad enough Gran lived with her and might be in the line of fire if the killer was looking at Maddie as the next victim.

"I know you all would have been there, but it was something I needed to do. Like I said, I did have Gran's help, and we all know how good her food is."

The other Girlz nodded in unison.

"Stop talking about food," Angel said. "My tummy is rumbling."

The others smiled affectionately at Angel, who looked like she survived on lettuce leaves, and often used food as a way of diffusing a difficult situation.

"We should tell Denise's parents that we'll see them there, then we can go." Maddie led the way over to the Loughlins, who she thought were being very brave.

The Loughlins hugged each of them, and Maddie's throat was tight with tears. Suzy came to the rescue.

"It was a lovely service. We're heading off to the hall to check on things."

"Thank you, girls," Mr. Loughlin said with a stiff smile.

"I know you've worked hard to make this a good sendoff for our little girl. We'll come by a little later."

After ensuring Gran was happy to come with her friends from the community center, the Girlz left before they could break down and upset the Loughlins further, and Angel handed out tissues as they sniffled their way to the hall. By the time they'd walked the few hundred feet, several others were already there. Fortunately, they were the ones who had offered to heat up the food and make tea and coffee, which had been done. Maddie need not have worried, but it had kept her mind busy.

Without discussion, the Girlz headed to a table-and-chair setting in the far corner and sat down with a collective sigh. The home-made tablecloths had been donated by the community center, and each had been hand-embroidered with a different flower. It was a lovely touch which softened the dark wood of the hall.

Maddie was about to put her bag on the floor when she noticed an envelope sticking out of it. A chill ran up her spine as she pulled it out. It was the same size and color as the one she'd received the day before. She could feel the color drain from her face.

"What's that?" Angel asked.

"Nothing." Maddie pushed it back into her bag with a shaking hand. She should have known the Girlz would see her anguish.

"What's going on?" Suzy demanded.

"I can't talk about it." Ignoring her bag, Maddie traced the pattern of a rose on the tablecloth.

"Can't, or won't?" Angel's tone was full of concern.

"Can't."

Suzy leaned in. "Is this something to do with the murder?"

Maddie meant to shake her head, but, to her dismay, she couldn't help but nod instead.

Angel moved her chair closer. "You have to tell us. Otherwise, we'll only assume the worst. Please."

Maddie sighed. As Denise's friends, they did have a right to know, and she trusted most of them to keep it to themselves. There was still a question mark after Laura's name.

"This letter—it isn't the first one I've received, and it wasn't in my bag before the funeral. I don't know how it got in there, but I'm pretty sure it'll be in the same vein as the last one."

Suzy leaned toward Maddie's bag, trying to get a better look. "And what vein would that be?"

"Threatening." Maddie's voice caught a little, and Angel put a hand on her arm.

"I can't believe this. Who would threaten you, and why?" Angel asked.

"That's the point. I have no idea."

Suzy pointed at the bag. "As scary as you're making this sound, I'm intrigued. Go ahead and open it. You'll have to eventually."

"I should wait for Ethan," Maddie said, even as she reached for it. The other three women craned their necks as she ripped it open. Maddie wished she had a similar enthusiasm, but how could she, when she had a pretty good idea of the contents? "It won't be anything good," she muttered, as the familiar scent hit her nostrils.

"Be positive. It could be a thank you note." Laura leaned over her shoulder.

If only it was something that pleasant. Maddie wanted to tell them to go away, to not get involved for their own safety, but she was scared to be alone with whatever this was. If only Ethan were here. The first thing she'd done after she'd found the envelope was to search the room for him.

With a shaking hand, she carefully undid the flap and pulled out the single sheet of paper by its edges. With a deep breath, she unfolded it, a sense of déjà vu hanging over her.

Chapter Nineteen

I told you to mind your own business. Go back to New York.

Angel picked the paper up from the floor where it had fallen from Maddie's numb fingers. She smoothed it out on her lap before Maddie could tell her to be careful of fingerprints.

"What the heck is this about?" Angel demanded.

She didn't get angry very often, but she was now, and her usually porcelain skin was a deep red. Laura and Suzy were pale by comparison as they bent over the note. Maddie wished she could take back that they knew. She should be tougher than this. Now they'd all be worried, and that was another burden.

"Someone must think I know who the murderer is. This is the second letter warning me to leave." Maddie shuddered. "I shouldn't be showing or telling you about this. I'm a terrible friend, getting all of you involved."

Angel made a rude sound. "Oh my goodness. You're right, this is awful, but if you're being threatened, how can I not be involved? I'm your best friend, aren't I?"

"The same goes for me," Suzy said firmly.

"And me," Laura added with a worried expression as she scanned the room.

"Thank you," Maddie told them, "but this could be a dangerous situation."

Suzy looked around. "There's nothing more dangerous than having a killer on the loose. He could be watching us right now."

"Or she," Angel said.

Maddie had been thinking about strangers as possible letter-senders. "Pardon me?"

"What makes you think it's a man and not a woman?" Suzy put her hands on her hips, ever the feminist.

"I guess I never considered it. You're right, it could very well be a woman," Maddie conceded.

The room had filled to capacity. There seemed to be more people here than at the funeral, which meant more strangers, and a greater chance one of them wasn't here to pay their respects.

"I promised to take a turn making tea and coffee. I hope I can do it without spilling everything. Look at me." Laura held her shaking hands out.

"Good luck. I'll come and give you a hand in a while," Angel told her.

Maddie sat back and clenched her fists. This wasn't how she'd intended to live her life. Running scared wasn't an option she cared to choose. Making a new life here with her bakery and being back with Gran and the Girlz was a change she knew was right, and she wouldn't be run out of town.

"Isn't it weird how the letter is typed?" Suzy asked.

Maddie nodded. "Very. Who even has a typewriter, let alone uses one?"

"Did you notice how the small 't' is missing the lower half?"

They looked at the note again and sure enough, it was.

Angel tilted her head. "Doesn't Mickey Findlay have one in his office at the front of his house? I remember going in there to talk to Anna Ramsey about her next appointment, and it was on a stand in the corner of the room among some other pieces of old things."

Maddie stared at her in amazement. "I might take a look for myself."

"I'll come with you."

"We don't want to make it seem as if we know anything."

"Well we don't know anything for sure and I'm the one with the lead."

Maddie took the paper and the envelope and put them in her bag. Then she took hold of Suzy's and Angel's hands

"I don't want anyone to get hurt because of me, but I do want the killer caught. For Denise, and for the town. Something like this affects us all. We shouldn't have to live in fear. The police have no real leads, so I'm going to do what I can to change that."

Angel thumped a delicate hand on the table. "I agree. Let's go find Ethan."

If this had been happening to any of them, she would want to help. Now she had little choice but to accept her friends were involved, and they would hound her until she did. But she could still protect the others, or at least try to.

Maddie grabbed her arm. "No. Listen to me. This has to be a covert operation. I'm going to find the killer. If you want to help, that's fine, but no one else. Not even Gran."

Angel gasped. "You're going to keep all this a secret from her?"

"She knows about the first letter. I don't want her to worry more than she already is. I'm not going to tell her about this one. Everything that's happened lately is taking a toll on her."

"It's your call, but she'll be plenty mad when she finds out."

Maddie knew without a doubt Gran would be furious, but she lifted her chin. "Let me deal with that if it comes up."

Suzy had gone a little pale. "I don't think we're equipped to be detectives, and Ethan will be even madder than Gran when he finds out we're snooping around. You could be subverting justice or interfering with an investigation."

Maddie hadn't thought about that. How could she protect Ethan if she told him? But if she didn't, and if because of it the killer got away, she wouldn't be able to forgive herself. This was tricky, but she felt a determination welling up inside her that was reminiscent of her move to New York City and wanting the bakery.

"Okay, Ms. Encyclopedia," she said. "We'll tell him about the letter, but not about us trying to help. If we get some real clues, we can hand them over to him."

"I don't know." Suzy was torn. "It sounds risky."

"Like I said before, you don't have to be a part of this. I totally understand that it's scary."

Suzy gave her a weak smile. "Yes, it is. Very scary and potentially illegal. But we're a team. Count me in."

"All right!" Angel actually did a fist pump.

They stood in a circle and hugged.

Maddie leaned in, as did the others, until their heads touched. "Okay," Maddie said. "Looks like we're doing this."

"So, what happens next?" Suzy asked.

"We go back to my place as soon as we can leave here and make a plan together."

A deep voice interrupted their huddle. "A plan for what?"

They wore their guilt like a bad costume. Blushing every shade of red and more than a little flustered, they began to talk at once. Ethan held up a hand and nodded to Maddie, and they couldn't help but hush.

"We're thinking about a cooking class," she said with her fingers crossed behind her back.

"Yes, that's it exactly. A cooking class!" Angel nodded a little too zealously.

"Wonderful idea, isn't it, Ethan?" Suzy added.

"Really? You have time for that?" He didn't look sold.

Angel was standing next to him, wide-eyed and taking her time searching for something plausible to say. Maddie nudged her.

"Uhhh, actually, it's something I asked Maddie to consider when she came home. We all suck at cooking, and it's time we addressed it."

Ethan raised an eyebrow. "Then maybe I should join you instead of relying on the goodwill of the town and my sister."

"No!" Again, it was a chorus, and Ethan regarded them suspiciously.

"We want it to be a close-knit, fun thing, and having a man around would cramp our style," Maddie explained.

Ethan had no choice but to surrender. "Seems a little sexist to me, but I wouldn't want to get in the way of women bonding. By the way, I thought you'd like to know that there've been a lot of compliments about the food. Well done, Maddie, and to you ladies for organizing things for the family. Denise was lucky to have you for friends."

Maddie blushed again. "Thanks, Ethan. She would have done the same for us."

"I have no doubt. Maddie, can I have a word?"

She hesitated at the coolness in his voice, but he had already moved away with a clear expectation she would follow him.

"Good luck," Angel said quietly.

Maddie followed him into the small, secluded yard behind the town hall. It had a maple tree in the far corner, creating shade and giving the impression there was a roof overhead, and a small fountain was trickling water over a trio of cherubs. The peace of the spot fell away when Ethan turned to her with a face like thunder.

"Where is it?"

She took a step back. "Pardon?"

"No games, Maddie. You received another letter, didn't you?"

"How did you know?"

He sighed heavily. "I could see you from across the room, showing the Girlz."

That didn't bode well. If Ethan had seen everything, the killer might have as well. She needed to get a lot better at this if she was going to get any results.

"I was going to tell you."

"You expect me to believe that?"

Her cheeks were hot. "Ask the Girlz if you don't."

"As if they'd tell me if you didn't want them to."

Maddie was insulted by his insinuation that she would ask them to lie for her. Then she saw reason. They would if they felt they had to. That was different. Right?

"I can't make them do anything they don't want to do.

166

I'm not Suzy." She hoped reminding him about Suzy being the sweet talker amongst them would lighten him up a little.

It didn't.

"No, you're not, but those women are incredibly loyal to you, and you darn well know it. Are you going to hand it over, or do I need to search you?"

Horrified, Maddie handed him her purse. "It's in there."

He held the black bag as awkwardly as if she'd handed him her underwear. "Just the letter would have done fine."

She tried for nonchalance while her heart pounded in her chest. This wasn't going according to her plan. It might be impossible to do anything quietly to help the investigation with such a determined sheriff in town.

"Help yourself."

His big hands were perfect for cutting wood or arresting people, but not so good for opening delicate bags. Frustrated, he pawed at the clasp and finally got it open. Carefully, he pulled out the envelope and the sheet of paper with two fingers.

"It's probably not going to give you any prints," she admitted. "Too many people have touched it."

He sighed. "Why did you let them? This is evidence."

"I didn't 'let them'. It was an accident. I was shocked, and I dropped it."

"You shouldn't have opened it in the first place. You should have called me as soon as you found it."

His censure had always been hard to take, especially when he was right. In fact, it was darn irritating that he constantly was right.

"I did look for you before I touched it."

"Not very hard, I'm guessing."

She lifted her chin. "I'm not the person you should be

interrogating. The Girlz saw it and wanted to know why I reacted like I did. I had to tell them."

"Maddie, listen to me. This is serious, and I don't want you taking any risks, either by yourself or with the Girlz. Okay?"

She appreciated what he was saying, but they hadn't found the murderer yet, had they? "Okay."

He didn't look like he particularly believed her, but he seemed a little less angry. "I'll leave you to your plans for the 'cooking club'." He handed her back her purse, then tucked the letter and the envelope into a plastic evidence bag and walked away with a shake of his handsome head.

She followed at a distance, and when she got back to the Girlz, they were watching his progress across the room.

"He's divine in that suit," Suzy sighed.

Angel snapped her fingers. "Honey, that man would be divine in anything. Or nothing."

Suzy nodded. "You're so lucky, Maddie."

Maddie rolled her eyes. "I've told all of you. We're friends. End of story."

The other women looked at each other and smiled. Clearly, Maddie wasn't about to win this argument anytime soon. That was one of the downfalls of living in a small town. People made a decision based on what they thought they knew, and you often couldn't get them to shake it.

"You told him about the note?" Angel asked.

"He knew. He saw us reading it," Maddie admitted. It was obvious her ability as an amateur sleuth was in question at this point.

"Darn, he's good," Suzy said with a grin.

"If he was that good, he would have caught the killer already, wouldn't he?"

"That's harsh, Maddie. Too harsh." Angel shook her head in disappointment.

"You're right. He's been harassing me lately, that's all. I know he's a good sheriff, but that's not to say he couldn't do with our assistance. You read the letter. I don't want him to get hurt on account of me."

"I'm guessing you didn't tell him about our typewriter theory, so we're going ahead with this despite him and his sexy cleverness?" Suzy asked.

Maddie gave a small grin. "Definitely. Let's mingle a little more and see if anyone has any interesting opinions on the murder they want to share. I'd bet everyone here is or has been discussing that very thing today. Just be sure not to speak to the family about it."

The Girlz nodded and spread out to find those people who always had something to say about others, with the exception of the group from the community center. Anything talked about with them would most certainly get back to Gran.

Maddie went to stand near the food tables. That seemed like the place everyone would turn up eventually, even those who were looking at her sideways. Funny how the food was being eaten anyway.

This had to be the longest day ever.

Chapter Twenty

Ethan tried to call Maddie over the next few days, but she made Gran answer the phone and say she was busy, which wasn't a total lie. Finally, he stood in her way at the grocery store. She turned to grab the closest item and study the contents.

"Hi, Maddie. How are you?"

"I'm fine, thank you. Excuse me, I'm in a rush."

He didn't budge. "Isn't the shop closed?"

"It is, but I have some orders to do tonight, and I need these ingredients." She pointed to her basket, avoiding looking at him.

He nodded at the product in her hand. "How does men's deodorant taste?"

She looked down, shocked to find the spray there. "Don't be silly. I just prefer it to women's."

He raised an eyebrow. "I see. Super-strength? Good to know. I was wondering if you'd like to have dinner this Saturday."

She hadn't seen that coming. If she said yes, she had the feeling he'd wear her down and she'd spill all the details of her investigation. She wondered what he'd uncovered, but she couldn't let that sway her.

"Sorry, I'm all booked up."

"You have a date?"

She frowned and tried to get past him. "Don't sound so shocked."

He put his hand on her arm. "What's gotten into you?"

"I have no idea what you're talking about."

"You're acting weird."

"You've always known I'm a little weird." She tried a joke as she made another attempt to get past.

He moved too. "'Frosty' would be more accurate. Ever since the funeral."

"Don't be silly. I'm busy, is all."

"Things were fine until a few days ago. When you got that second letter and stopped taking my calls."

"I've been trying to get my business on its feet, and there's been a murder."

He sighed, a sound that was heavy with exasperation. "I'm only too aware, since it's my job to solve it. What's your point?"

"For goodness' sake, whoever did it is watching you and me. I think it's smart to stay away from each other for the time being."

"That's all it is? You aren't avoiding me for any other reason?"

"What reason?"

He raised his eyebrows, and she looked into her basket.

"Ethan, we've barely seen each other for years, we can hardly...you know."

"What? Talk?"

His teasing wasn't what she needed right now. "Pretend we're the same people we were back then."

"I know we're not. Which is a good thing, don't you think?"

Maddie's heart fluttered. "Yes, I guess it is. It means we can move on from each other in a friendly way."

Ethan took a step back, and his expression shut down. "If that's really how you feel, then excuse me for keeping you."

This wasn't what she'd intended. Or was it? She had to push him away until she had more evidence. "See you around."

He shook his head at her, and she felt as though she'd let him down. She squared her shoulders. A man who looked like Ethan was sought after by all the single women, locals and tourists alike. He'd be just fine.

But she'd hate to lose him as a friend now that they'd cleared the air. When this was all done, she'd make it up to him—if he gave her the chance. He might be upset now, but he was going to feel a lot worse when he found out she was going rogue.

Best not to think about that until she couldn't avoid it. She really needed to bake something. Right now.

"Maddie, are you okay? You look like you're going to pass out. Have you been out in the sun without a hat? Or was our sheriff bugging you?"

Angel had taken Ethan's place, and Maddie licked her dry lips as she looked around the store.

"No, but I can't be seen with him right now." Just then she caught sight of someone hovering nearby. "It's been a hot day, hasn't it? I'm about to do some baking, and I'll need every fan I have to get it done."

Angel followed her gaze and she nodded. "Make sure you drink plenty of water."

"Yes, ma'am." Maddie saluted as they headed to the

counter to pay for their shopping. Then they walked outside into the afternoon sunshine.

The store was opposite the park, where Noah was teaching his Sunday yoga class. Laura was in the front row with Suzy, and they were both getting tangled as they concentrated more on their tutor than on what they were supposed to be doing.

"He gets better-looking every time I see him," Angel noted.

"How come you're not in the class? I thought yoga was a passion of yours."

"It is, and normally I would be, but I had to find you. I didn't need a thing from the store." Angel produced a folded piece of paper from her white linen pants as if she were a magician. "It's a list from the guest book which was at the funeral. Most of the guests would have put their names in it," she said softly.

"This is awesome. Do you want to come back to my place, and we can go over it?"

Angel looked at her watch. "Sure. It's too late to join the class, and I'm hungry. Do you have leftovers?"

Maddie laughed. Although the reason for Angel to come home with her was morbid, her friend was always a tonic for the downside of life. "Can a fish swim?" she asked.

They walked around the park and crossed over to Maddie's bakery, but went around the back to the kitchen entrance.

Every day since the funeral, Angel (sometimes with Suzy) had come to the apartment, where they utilized every available moment to pore over each scrap of evidence linked to the murder and talk about what had happened at the funeral. There wasn't a lot, since Maddie had no input from the police, but the list Angel had might be invaluable and their first chance to find proper leads. They'd have to fill Suzy in later. It helped that Gran had been spending more time in the evening and on weekends house packing, so they didn't have to explain things, or worse, hide what they were doing from her.

"How did you get hold of the guest book?" Maddie asked.

"I was visiting the Loughlins and saw the book on their table. I asked to look through it, and when they were out of the room, I took photos of each page. I typed it up at home, so we can move things around if we need to. This is the result."

"Well done! I didn't know you were so sneaky. I've been nervous to ask around too much because we don't know who's involved. I was going to chat with the cashiers at the store today, but our sheriff got in the way of that."

"He does turn up when you least expect it. I guess that makes him the sneakiest."

Maddie grinned. "True. Anyway, back to the list. It could be one person or many, but if we group the names of our suspects, we might find connections we haven't thought of."

"How do we define a group?"

Maddie had already considered that, and she pulled the notebook she'd taken to carrying around with her out of her bag. "For a start, we can have one list for people who've said or done something negative towards Denise before or after her death. Then another one for who they associate with. Maybe one for those we think don't abide by the law?"

"Apart from a few incidents which were written up in the paper, everybody seems to have behaved since the murder."

Maddie shook her head. "Not everyone. I have two notes suggesting otherwise."

Angel gave her a measured look. "All right. Let's start at the beginning. What do we have, Sherlock?"

"We have a pie competition, a murder by poison, and two letters."

"Motives?" Angel was also ready with a pad and pen she'd grabbed from Maddie's desk.

"Anger over the results of the competition. A lover's quarrel. Potentially political. Jealous about accomplishments. The admirer was jilted."

Angel frowned. "I can't imagine anyone killing Denise over not receiving a ribbon at the fair."

"It is kind of far-fetched, but there were some rumblings about me entering, so it's a possibility." Maddie had a flashback of Laura talking to the Blue Brigade. What had she said to them?

Oblivious to where Maddie's thoughts were traveling, Angel scribbled furiously. "I heard them, and I've circled the people who might have instigated the complaints or bought into them. What else?"

Maddie wrote that down as one thing she wouldn't have to tackle. "Do you know if Denise was seeing anyone apart from this admirer? She certainly didn't mention being interested in a man to me."

Angel chewed a long pink nail. "She hasn't had so much as one date. Not since Ethan."

Maddie felt the color drain from her face. "Pardon me?"

"Oh my goodness. You didn't know?" Angel clapped a hand over her mouth.

Maddie shook her head. "No, I didn't. When was this, and why didn't you tell me?"

"It was during the election. I figured Denise or Ethan

might have said something. Especially with you and Ethan getting friendly again."

"Well, that's all it is. When I left, we were done, and I haven't changed my mind. Besides, I'd never be interested in someone else's man."

"He was hardly that, and not to be indelicate, but Denise is gone."

Maddie shuddered. "That's beside the point."

"I don't think it is. It was over months ago, and it was just a brief thing. Denise was too wrapped up in her job, and Ethan hasn't gotten serious about anyone since you."

"Stop it, Angel. I'm still upset you didn't say anything, and if not you, then Gran should have told me."

"I'm sorry. You had a boyfriend, so I guess we didn't think it was important." Angel looked upset.

Maddie hated that look. Angel didn't deserve her censure, because she was right—it shouldn't matter. "You're right. It isn't a big deal. I'm only feeling bad because I didn't have a clue and it made me feel out of the loop. Being away from you all, I was happy enough knowing you girls would keep me up to date with things. We've always told each other everything. Or we used to."

Angel was still flushed, but she brought them back on track. "We could go around in circles over it, but it's too late to change things, and Denise is still gone. Why don't we get back to these names? The book had a column where the guests could put down where they were from, or their connection to Denise, and I put all that on the list. Look at this one: Marie Loughlin. Portland. Much-loved cousin."

Maddie was still wondering how Denise and Ethan had hooked up, but time was ticking by, and so far, they had nothing to show for it but these lists. Angel had two copies, and she passed one over to Maddie. It had been marked up with several different-colored highlighters. "What are these colors for?"

Angel laid out her set of highlighters in a row in front of her. "I think we should use different colors to show who we think is a likely candidate, a not possible, and everything in between."

Color was Angel's thing, and it made sense. "It's as good a system as any, I guess," Maddie said. "Tell me what colors you've picked for each group, and I'll get started."

Angel consulted her key. "Red for possible. Green, no way. Orange for a slight chance, and gold for I bet they did it."

Maddie couldn't help letting out a laugh. Angel had that effect, even when life was a mess.

She went through the list and, as best she could, gave a reason each name should stay or go. The one name Maddie had to struggle with was Laura's. No matter that she was Angel's friend; Maddie had an odd feeling Laura knew something. There were several reasons she wasn't willing to share with Angel, since she didn't think her friend would view them in an unbiased light, and those she chose to put on a separate page.

1. She was badmouthing or listening to badmouthing about me in the contest tent.

2. She was at Denise's earlier that day.

3. She doesn't really like me and seems jealous of my relationship with Angel.

4. She was a rival for the mayor's position.

5. She's reluctant to help search for the murderer.

6. She also entered an apple pie in the contest.

That was more than what they had on anyone else. Maddie tucked the page in the back, determined to look into the Laura situation when she was alone.

An hour later, they each had a colorful document. "Let's marry them up," Maddie said, then placed hers along-side Angel's. They found a lot of similarities. "I see we both have Virginia as the lead suspect."

Angel nodded eagerly. "Naturally. She doesn't like anyone, but she hated Denise."

Maddie was surprised. "Hated? I know she's not a nice person, but that's a strong word."

"True, and it's not one I generally like to use. The story was, they had that major fallout at school and another when Denise got elected as mayor. Virginia wanted the job real bad. In fact, she told anyone who'd listen that she had it in the bag. Now, I know that's a metaphor, but somebody found a bag with a whole stack of ballots inside. Guess whose name was on all of them?"

"No way!"

"Way. Virginia Bolton. Let me just say that the you-know-what hit the fan. The whole town vilified her for weeks. It was only Denise, being the bigger person, telling us there was no proof Virginia was the culprit and it was irrelevant now, that caused everyone to calm down. Person-ally, I never got my head around the fact Virginia might have been mayor."

Maddie took in every word, stunned at getting all this information from Angel, who had never spoken this way about anyone—although she certainly had every right to, considering the way some people had treated her, especially Virginia.

In a town as small as theirs, where gossip ran rife, it was amazing that Maddie had been here for months without anyone telling her any of this. Especially Ethan, Angel, and Suzy—and even Denise. Then there was Gran. Maddie made a mental note to have a word with her later. "I had no idea the mayoral race was fought so hard."

Angel nodded. "Actually, there were three people who wanted the job. Denise, Virginia, and Laura."

"Why did Laura want to be mayor here?"

"Her parents heard of the opening through Mickey Findlay and thought she would have an easy shot at it. That was before Denise decided to run. Laura worked hard to promote herself, but she didn't know anywhere near enough people even with the Findlay's backing. Most people voted for Denise. A few might have actually voted for Virginia, but that didn't leave many for poor Laura."

"Why did she stay after she'd lost."

Angel smiled. "She'd already fallen in love with Maple Falls. I was delighted when she decided to stay. I think I told you how we hit it off when she came to O'Malley's one night. There was a band. She was new in town, and a little shy, and I could see she was itching to dance. You know how I like to dance, so the rest was history."

Angel, Suzy and Maddie had all been dancing queens back in the day. It still gave Maddie a pang to think of Angel having fun with a new bestie, but that was wrong of her. She understood how hard it was to leave your friends and try to make new ones.

So, Laura had been lonely? Maddie didn't know her well at all, and to be honest, hadn't made much of an effort. And she had more questions.

"She came from L.A., didn't she?"

"That's right."

"Does she have other friends here? Did she know anyone before she turned up?"

"No, she didn't know anyone, and she has us." Angel suddenly slapped her pen on the table. "Wait a cotton-picking minute. I was giving you some background, not putting her name forward as a suspect. See, she's green on my list. And you have her as—orange? She told me once that you don't like her. Now I see it's true."

There was a world of hurt in her friend's eyes, and Maddie tried to make her voice sound reasonable and light. "Angel, if we're going to do this right, we have to consider everyone. Not just the people we like. Even I was a suspect."

"Sure, for all of five minutes. Tell me truthfully. Do you like Laura?"

Telling the truth could sometimes be one heck of a burden, Maddie thought. "I don't dislike her. We're very different people."

Angel took a moment to digest that. "She said you were jealous of our friendship."

Maddie thought she could answer that honestly. "I knew you were friends, long before I came home this time, and I've tried to include her in everything we do. I admit to wanting to have you to myself sometimes, but isn't that reasonable? You and I go way back, and it's nice to have some things the way they were. I'm sorry if it's made her feel bad."

Angel sat back. "Maybe you should tell her that yourself."

"I will," Maddie promised.

"Then, let's talk about the rest of the people on our lists. Ones who aren't so upsetting to accuse, even on paper."

She was still clearly upset by Maddie's reasoning, but what else could Maddie say? She didn't want to put Laura down in front of Angel or make her best friend feel like she had to choose.

What a day.

Chapter Twenty-One

Wﬁith the air still frosty, Maddie and Angel
continued with their detective work. They
managed to steer clear of the elephant in the
room—Laura—as they did research on the names of people
in the book for motives and likeliness to commit murder,
shifting them from one list to another.

One name intrigued Maddie because he wasn't on the
list. She'd added him along with the other people she could
remember attending the funeral, but hadn't written in the
book.

Mickey Findlay, the descendant of a founding father,
was a man who bought and sold big developments all
around Portland. He was mega rich and looked like he had
every intention of becoming richer if he had his way. Inter-
estingly, he'd tried but failed to buy the large parcel of land
near town which had been used for years as the place where
festivals and market days where held. The land had been
gifted to the town to ensure there was always such a place.
The last attempt, was during Denise's tenure and not that

long ago. It might be nothing, but it was certainly worth looking into.

"I've been meaning to stop by Mr. Findlay's office to check on that typewriter, but I can't think of a way to do it."

"You're looking tired, Maddie. How about I do it. Anna's a client so it's not strange that I would visit her."

Even though she was annoyed with Maddie, Angel could never stay angry or aloof.

"I am exhausted," she admitted. "With the baking, and all this extra work, I don't have a spare minute, but I'm determined to find the killer."

"I feel the same way, except my business hasn't been affected like yours. Hopefully that's changing?"

Maddie pushed her hair back from her face. "Apparently, according to a few, my food might still be poisoning the whole town." She gave Angel a small smile.

"Don't joke. I know it's nonsense, and so do most people."

"That's not enough. Sales haven't picked up to anywhere near what they were that first week. I haven't told Gran how worried I am."

"Laura suggested an ad in the paper, maybe from the health department, saying your food is safe?"

Maddie's mouth gaped for a second. "Laura did?"

Angel frowned. "She's trying to help."

"Is she?" The words slipped out, and Maddie wanted to take them back immediately.

Naturally, Angel took exception. "Okay, this has to stop. It's not my place to tell you her story, but I'm going to do it anyway."

Maddie sat back, wondering what on earth Angel could say that would make a difference in what she already knew.

"Laura didn't really want to be mayor. Anyone who

listened to her speeches could have picked up on that and would have thought voting for her was a waste of time."

Maddie was surprised by Angel's comments about her friend, but there was more.

"The only reason she ran for office was because her family pushed her into it. Her parents are bullies who turned ugly when she didn't win despite all the money they threw at it. They called her a failure to her face and told her she was on her own."

"Laura's family really threw her out because she didn't win?"

"That's right. They're rich, but what they want is to be associated with important people. They thought their daughter would be that ticket."

"Wow, they sound like a fun family."

"Exactly. Laura isn't like them. She doesn't want to be noticed, which is why she loves our town. People talk to her because she's nice, not because her parents have money and they want something from her. She's also here because she had nowhere else to go."

"That's terrible."

"Yes, it is." Angel gave Maddie a sideways look. "Everyone has their own story. You and I have had our issues with family. Don't you think it's right that we should be more understanding?"

Her friend's insight hit Maddie between the eyes. "You're right. I should have tried harder to know her."

Angel smiled. "I'm glad you agree. Now, show me the darn list you have for her."

Maddie's mouth dropped open. "Shoot. You know about it?"

"You're the queen of lists. For sure you have to have one on Laura. One you thought I shouldn't see."

Maddie reluctantly pulled the sheet of paper from her file. "Here you go. Don't hate me."

"No promises."

Angel read through it, making rude noises throughout. "Okay, I'm going to tackle these one by one. Are you ready to really listen?"

"Sure," Maddie said. And she was. For the first time, she truly wanted to be wrong about Laura.

Angel began to read and answer each point.

"'1. She was badmouthing or listening to badmouthing about me in the contest tent.' Laura told me about the old biddies talking about you, and she said she told them the best was the best, no matter who made it. Then she walked away.

"'2. She was at Denise's earlier that day.' Laura was having breakfast with Denise to talk about the food donations because she was the one who started up the program, and she wanted to stay involved even though she hadn't won the election.

'3. She isn't friendly to me and she seems jealous my relationship with Angel.' If Laura seems like she doesn't like you, it's because she thought you don't like her. I don't get the jealousy thing because I know I can love plenty of people.

'4. She was a rival for the Mayor's position.' This is absolutely true, but she didn't want the job. She was a terrible candidate and couldn't speak to crowds. I'd bet a years' worth of doughnuts no one could fake that level of relief.

'5. She's reluctant to help search for the murderer.' Laura never said she wouldn't help, but she's also a lot more nervous than you or me. She would have made a terrible mayor, because she actually hates confrontation. Again, this is a trait she learned from having horrible parents. I might add that she's been doing stuff behind the scenes for me.

'6. She also entered an apple pie in the contest.' Hmmm. Now, this I don't get. If it was a stranger, maybe, but I spent a lot of time with her before and after the election. I think I'd know if she had some hidden agenda, but all I saw was a person who genuinely liked Denise and that was reciprocated. Plus, all the contestants were cleared of having poison in their entries."

She folded her arms and waited.

It was a lot to digest, but Maddie trusted Angel, and having this out in the open meant she didn't have to hide her feelings.

"Are you still unsure?" Angel asked. "Is there anything else I can help clear up?"

Maddie shook her head. "No, you've convinced me. Laura isn't the killer. And I should have listened to you before this and trusted your judgment."

Angel beamed. "That makes me happy. Now, we've decided I'll visit Anna, so what's next?" She brushed her hands together, as if she had finished baking something.

Maddie felt something shift a little. Having your best friend mad at you could make life unbearable. Having her forgive you without you saying you were sorry was a testament to their friendship.

Chapter Twenty-Two

When Gran's or Maddie's loyal friends did come into the shop, the conversation was invariably about the murder. Maddie forced herself to encourage it, despite the jab to the stomach she felt each time Denise's death was mentioned. At least this way she could hear people's opinions firsthand, and she and Angel had already ticked a few people off the list after they were mentioned as being elsewhere.

Angel was doing the same in her salon, Suzy in her various meetings at the school, and Laura at O'Malley's. The list was getting smaller, but there were still too many names on it to point fingers.

Maddie, up early as usual, had some pies underway she wanted herbs for. She went out back to her garden, which was doing wonderfully. With a pair of small scissors, she cut off oregano, parsley and thyme... and promptly dropped them when she saw another envelope tucked against the back door.

Maddie snatched it up, looking around her. There were

no cars or people on Plum Place. It was a quiet, serene morning. At least it had been.

After picking up the fallen herbs, she went inside and shut the door. She laid the herbs in the sink to wash, then called out to Gran, who was in the shop. "I'm just going upstairs for a minute." Not waiting for a reply, she took the stairs two at a time, went into the small kitchen, grabbed some gloves, then headed to her bedroom and closed the door. She sat on the edge of her bed. Without giving herself time to dwell on the contents, she ripped it open.

I guess you don't care what happens to you. Don't say I didn't warn you.

Did that mean the killer knew what she and the Girlz were doing? Did it mean they were close? And what should she do about it? All three letters were threatening, but nothing bad had actually happened. She would have to give it some thought before she said anything to Ethan. He would come by more often, not less, if he knew, which kind of defeated the purpose of her trying to protect him.

She tucked the envelope into the back of her underwear drawer, then went downstairs to finish the pies, determined to not let this latest note affect her. Or at least not show that it was.

A while later, she was loading a pile of chocolate chip cookies into the display case when Laura came into the shop. Gran had recently pulled some scones out of the industrial oven, and she came through the curtain at the same time.

"Morning, Laura," she called out as she slid the tray of scones into the display case. Then she gave Maddie a frown and nodded at Laura.

Laura didn't look like herself. She was usually smartly

dressed whether she was working or not, but today she looked unkempt and tired.

"Morning. How are you, Mrs. Flynn?" Laura asked Gran.

"It's time you called me Gran. Everyone does, even those who are far too old to do so. I'm doing much better, thank you. I still feel shocked about Denise, but I'm sure the whole town feels the same way."

Laura became tearful. "I know I do, and I didn't know her as long as the rest of you. Lately, we'd been seeing a lot of each other, and I considered her a good friend." There was an awkward pause, then Laura took a huge breath. "I know I look rough, but I had to see you, Maddie. I've really upset Angel."

Maddie went from awkward to angry in two seconds. "What have you done?"

"She asked me about being jealous of you, and I couldn't lie. I knew Angel was putting the blame mostly at your door for our not getting along, but I also know I haven't made it easy for you because, really, I was jealous. I'm ashamed about that, and with what's happened—is there a chance we could put it behind us?"

Her anger melted instantly. It took a lot for someone to admit they were wrong, and Laura was showing great strength and humility in doing so. Maddie owed it to Angel to resolve the bad feeling, and if their friendship was going to get back to where it had once been, this was the perfect place to start.

Gran fussed with the display cases, and Maddie could almost feel the waves of encouragement coming off her.

"Laura, I'm sorry too. I was wrong. I judged you without taking the time to get to know you. It should have been enough that you are Angel's friend."

"You had every right to think bad things about me. I wasn't myself the few times we met before you came home. The election took more of a toll than I thought it would, and my family was upset about the whole business. It made me angry and resentful because I felt like I was useless at everything."

Maddie didn't want to let on that Angel had told her about Laura's family. "Angel hangs on to her friends even when they don't deserve it. Look at me."

Laura laugh softly. "I wish I was like you. Fearless and talented." She sighed. "There's that jealousy again."

Maddie smiled. "No need for any of that. I'm sorry I haven't included you in the group as much as I should have. I have nothing against you personally. I suppose I wanted things to go back to the way they were before I left. It was wrong and selfish of me. What we need is a fresh start. There's always room for another friend, and I hope we'll be good ones."

Laura wiped the corners of her eyes and gave Maddie a wide smile. "You have no idea how that makes me feel. I thought it was something about me that was making you wary. I know I can be a little needy, but I was incredibly lonely when I first came here. It was important for me to make friends as soon as possible, mainly because of the election, and that's never been easy for me. When Angel extended her hand, I grabbed it like a lifeline. Then you came home, and I was afraid I'd be alone again. I never meant to come between you and Angel."

It made perfect sense to Maddie. When she moved to New York City, she'd known no one. If it hadn't been for her work colleagues, she wouldn't have had anyone to talk to for months. Angel had a talent for making a person feel cared about.

Gran wiped her face on the corner of her floral apron. "Angel has good taste when it comes to friends, so you must be all right."

Tears were rolling down Laura's cheeks. "Look at me. I'm a mess."

"I think you look fine." Maddie fetched some tissues and gave Laura a hug, then wiped her own eyes.

"It's a shame you don't have a coffee machine," Laura teased. "I could sure do with one."

"Ha! You can practically see it gathering dust right there." Maddie pointed to the end of the counter, where the fancy coffeemaker was covered with a tablecloth. "I read the manual, but it was all gibberish, and the coffees I made were hideous. So I refuse to make them. It's so frustrating, because most of our customers want a latte or a cappuccino, and all I can give them is one from the coffeepot."

"Should I give you a lesson? I was a barista, after all."

Maddie gaped at Laura. "What? How did I not know this?"

Laura shrugged. "I guess we've never talked about our past before."

Maddie had to agree. "It's a shame you have a job. I'd hire you in a flash."

Laura's grin slipped, and a light hit her eyes. "Are you serious? Don't say you are if you don't mean it, because I would love a job here."

Maddie shot Gran a look and received a nod of encouragement and a grin in return. This would mend so many fences.

"I mean it one hundred per cent. I know the machine is necessary, but without staff, I couldn't do it all anyway. I need you."

Laura's eyes widened, and she was on the verge of tears

again. "If you really do mean it, then I'd love the job. I hate working at O'Malley's. The different shifts mean I don't get to see Angel as much as I'd like, and I couldn't help with your lists."

Maddie hesitated, and Laura saw it.

She frowned. "Look, if you're having second thoughts, I totally understand."

Maddie shook her head. "It's not that. I can't pay much. I was looking at taking on a trainee, but business will be better with the coffees we can sell. The only downside is I really need another baker. Anyway, that's not your problem, but the money might be."

Laura wasn't perturbed. "I'd need enough for my rent and food. I wouldn't expect a huge salary to start."

Gran, who'd been listening closely, spoke up. "I have an idea. It might be temporary, but if you like, you can stay at my place until it's sold. I hate the thought of it being empty, but it makes no sense for me to stay there when Madeline needs me here."

"Oh! Yes, please, Mrs. Flynn. This is too perfect."

"You can't stay unless you call me Gran."

Laura flushed with pleasure. "Thank you, Gran."

Maddie smiled at them. "This is great. Now, if I could find a junior baker, this day would be perfect."

Laura opened her arms. "Teach me. There'll be times when no one wants coffee, and before the shop opens. I can work as many hours as you need me to for the same rate you'd pay a trainee."

"You'd be willing to learn from scratch?"

"I'd love it. One thing Angel and I have in common is we're useless cooks. We were talking about learning. She said you were going to teach her sometime and that I could learn from her. Maybe it could be the other way around."

Maddie had never seen Laura so excited, and she had more to say.

"Baking would be a good start, and I love everything you make. Plus, I can wash dishes. I imagine by giving people coffee and tea, they'll be dining in more, and therefore there'll be all those plates and cups."

"I love your enthusiasm. I anticipated a lot of dirty dishes, and I did put in a dishwasher when we redid the kitchen, so Gran and I wouldn't always be at the sink. I think it'll be earning its keep and all this sounds too good to be true. When can you start?"

"Today?" Gran gave Laura a hopeful grin.

Laura laughed. "Much as I'd like to, I have to give notice, or my name will be mud around town. How's next week? I'll still come by and show you how to work the machine if you want to use it beforehand."

"Perfect," Maddie and Gran said together. "Tea?"

"What's going on here?" Angel stood at the open back door.

"Maddie offered me a job, and I'm going to house sit at Grans until she sells."

Laura's excitement was catching, and Angel ran to throw her arms around Maddie, then the others.

"This is such good news. Although I did offer you my spare room ages ago."

Laura blushed. "You would have had to suffer my parents visiting and I would have been mortified to have you hear how they talk about me. I don't think they'll be coming anytime soon now they know how I feel."

"As long as you're happy, that's all I care about, and a person would have to be blind not to see that you are!"

"I am. But I should go and get ready for work."

"I'm off home for a bit to sort out your room, so I'll walk you out," said Gran.

Angel waited until they were alone before grabbing Maddie in a bear hug.

"Thank you, Maddie. You have made my day as well as Laura's."

Maddie blushed and squirmed. "It was purely selfish."

Angel laughed. "Uh huh. Sure, it was. Anyway, I went over to see Anna at Mickey Findlay's office."

Maddie was astounded. "Already? Did you look at the typewriter?"

"I sure did. I asked Anna if it still worked and she showed me it did. Look."

She handed Maddie a piece of paper with a rather smug expression. On it the words 'two talented women,' were typed. Half of the 't' was missing.

"This is proof that the letters came from him."

"Maybe, but how do we prove he was actually the one using it?"

Her heart sank. "You have a point. It's a start though. Thanks Angel."

"I have to run sweetie, but we'll talk some more soon."

After she left Maddie put the piece of paper with the letters, except for the one upstairs. How could they tie everything together?

Chapter Twenty-Three

Aslap across her face brought Maddie awake. Someone was in her bed. On her chest.

Slap!

She bolted upright, and Big Red let out a loud, outraged meow, as he rolled off her.

"Darn it. I was having the best sleep ever. What is wrong with you?" she coughed, then coughed again. A smell like something burning was wafting around her. *Wait!* It was smoke.

A loud wail made her leap out of bed. Thank goodness she'd installed the smoke alarm. The hall was narrow and took only a couple of steps to cross. Gran's door felt cool, and Maddie couldn't see any flames as she burst through into the room. She found Gran sitting up in bed, looking as disoriented as Maddie had been moments before.

"What's happening, sweetheart? Is that the smoke alarm? Is it us?"

"It is. I think the fire must be downstairs."

Gran got out of bed and put on a robe over her nightie.

"Oh dear. Not your beautiful shop. I was sure we turned everything off."

Maddie swallowed hard at the thought of what might be awaiting them. "Come on. We need to get out of here."

She had to wait for Gran to put on slippers.

"Follow me while I see if it's safe to go all the way down."

"I darn well hope so. I'm not climbing out a window. No siree!"

Maddie took her arm and led her adamant Gran to the stairwell. There was a lot more smoke there, but still no flames she could see.

Gingerly, they went down the stairs and into the kitchen. The alarm was so loud there that they held their hands to their ears. Big Red's hackles had risen to the extent that he looked like a ginger ball of fluff.

The back door was burning, flames creeping up the wall near the industrial oven. The fire extinguisher was on the wall opposite the door.

Maddie pushed Gran through into the shop with a damp dishcloth to her face and handed her the phone. "Get outside then call the fire department."

While Gran did this, Maddie wrestled the extinguisher from its clips. Pulling the pin, she sprayed the flames closest to the oven, coughing so hard it felt like her lungs would burst.

She had managed to push the fire back when she heard the shop door crash open and Ethan came flying through the curtain like a superhero, minus the cape and leotard.

They stood gaping at each other in relief for a few seconds until he snapped out of it. Snatching the extinguisher from her grip, he continued to beat back the flames.

He was still struggling when the fire department swarmed inside with heavy duty extinguishers and pushed the three of them outside through the shop before they set about dousing the last of the flames.

Ethan put down the empty canister and wiped his brow with his sleeve, smearing ash down his face. "Are you okay?"

Maddie retreated to where Gran was standing with Angel. She put her arm around her, thankful that she was safe but angry this had happened. There was no way this was an accident.

"After being wakened from a deep sleep by Big Red and being nearly burnt to a crisp in our beds? No, I'm not okay." Then she calmed down a bit. "Still, I'm so glad he woke me and that the damage isn't any worse. Imagine if after all our hard work, the whole place had burned to the ground." Maddie began to shake, knowing she was babbling and unable to control it.

Gran had one arm around Maddie's waist while her other hand held her robe tightly together. Maddie glanced down at her own flimsier attire, a long white t-shirt with *Don't wake me, I'm dreaming* written across the front that barely skimmed her thighs.

Ethan saw her embarrassment and took off his jacket to put it around her. She didn't refuse, even if it did smell of smoke. She almost laughed at the notion of being picky, because she could now smell her own hair as it fell around her face. The escaping blonde strands from her braid fairly reeked. Hysteria felt as close to her as the flames had been.

"Do we know how the fire started?" she asked, her voice higher than usual.

Ethan looked at the burly fire chief, Ryan Jones, who had left the dampening down of the area to his crew while he surveyed the damage. The chief seemed reluctant to answer the question, but Ethan motioned for him to speak.

"Arson?" he asked.

Still reluctant, the chief said, "It's possible. There are traces of an accelerant near the back door. But we'll need to do a full investigation before we can make a determination."

Ethan nodded. "Keep me informed."

"The investigation will take a while," Chief Jones said to Maddie. "We'll need you to stay somewhere else for the rest of the night."

"That's not a problem, my house is just down the street, but could we go upstairs to get some clothes?" Gran asked him in a small voice.

"I'm sorry, the arson investigator will need to check the property to make sure the structure is safe, and the smoke will not clear properly for some time. One of my men will go with you."

"I can take Gran to the cottage, if you're not ready, Maddie," Angel offered.

"Thanks. I won't be long." She waited for Gran, Angel and the chief to walk away before she turned to Ethan. "Why are you here?"

"I was passing by and saw the fire." His cheek twitched.

"Ethan, it's too late for a casual stroll. What were you really doing?"

He looked around, avoiding her eyes. "Don't be mad, but I've been keeping an eye on you."

"Every night?"

"Mostly."

She tapped her foot. "What do you mean?"

"I have a patrol come by several times, day and night."

"Since when?"

"Since the murder. It felt like someone was framing

you. I didn't say anything because I didn't want to alarm you any more than necessary."

Now she was just plain mad. "You don't get to tell me how or when to be scared. I'm a big girl, not the frightened one who went off to New York City on her own."

"I know you're not. The thing is, I can't help worrying about you. We have a history, and it was mostly good. It's not so easy to forget that you mattered."

Maddie was struck by how he'd changed. He'd been a painfully shy and awkward, skinny kid, until high school, when he began to fill out. One of the things that had made it easier to leave him was that he'd never professed love for her or anything even close to that. Now he was a hunk, and he didn't seem to have a problem with speaking his mind.

Her instinct to be grateful was stronger than the urge to throw something at him, but she was still annoyed.

"We were kids back then. Now we're adults, and I can take care of myself."

"Ordinarily I'd agree with you, but this is no ordinary thing that's happened, and coming right after the murder, I don't think I overreacted. Do you?"

If he hadn't arrived when he had, could she have put out the fire before it spread? Probably not. Which meant she might not have had a shop to open tomorrow. "I guess not. I'd better check on Gran. Thanks for being here and helping with the fire, Ethan."

Maddie felt bad for treating him this way, but she had no other choice.

Ethan took a step back. He had several streaks of ash running down his face, but she could clearly see he was just as annoyed as she was.

"Something's going on with you, and I don't like it." He

threw that into the space between them before he walked away.

She couldn't think of anything to say to stop him that wouldn't endanger him. What if the killer was watching them right now?

Chapter Twenty-Four

It was Monday, several days after the fire. Laura was starting work at the bakery today. The coffee machine was set up and ready to go.

Maddie spent Sunday getting her new staff member up to speed with the cash register and prices, and Laura had christened the machine, making them both the most delicious lattes. Laura had given Maddie and Gran a tutorial on how to use it and surprisingly the results had tasted nearly as wonderful as hers.

Gran grudgingly declared that even though it wasn't tea, it would be okay for the customers who didn't know what was good for them—and it would also save some wear and tear on her tea sets.

It had actually been a lot of fun, and they had seen another side of the usually serious Laura.

When she arrived at six for her introduction to the baking schedule, Laura was excited and eager to begin. Maddie had been up earlier to make and set the bread dough to rest, and Gran had made the usual scones and muffins, so the timing was perfect.

"Thanks so much for coming early," Maddie said. "You won't have to after today. Otherwise, it can be an awfully long day."

Laura waved a hand. "I'm always awake by now. I guess that makes me a morning person, and I'm happy to be busy."

"You sound just like me. Who would have thought?"

They smiled at each other.

"Say, the paint fumes have almost gone," Laura noted happily.

"Thank goodness! When I had to repaint this part of the kitchen after the fire I was worried about how you'd cope if it was still lingering, but you seem a lot better," Maddie said.

Laura smiled. "Honestly, I was too, but even since yesterday, there's a huge difference in here. I didn't like to admit it was affecting me because I really wanted the position. I haven't ever been this enthusiastic about any job."

Maddie could see and feel her sincerity. There was always the worry that if things turned sour it would upset everything with Angel, but she couldn't think about that now.

If they got along as well as they had over the last week, Maddie would be delighted. Laura was much nicer than she'd thought, even after their heart-to-heart. It was funny what festered away in people's minds, when an honest conversation and spending some time together could fix all that.

Now she felt guilty. She still hadn't told Ethan about the last letter. To take her mind off that swing of the pendulum, she began to show Laura how to make basic cookies. As they took them out of the oven, Angel came through the back door wearing a yellow dress.

"Look at you, baking and everything. They look delicious."

Laura grinned. "I made the uglier ones."

"They look good enough to me." Angel stole one from the tray, juggling it in her fingers, but the heat didn't stop her from taking a bite. "Mmmm. So good," she mumbled.

Gran was cleaning the counter they rolled everything out on, and she called out to Angel. "I don't know how you manage to look the way you do first thing in the morning, but today you look like sunshine. You three come and have a cup of tea or make yourselves some coffee and sit down for a few minutes before we open. It may be the last chance anyone gets for a while."

Gran stuck with her tea but Laura made the rest of them lattes. Angel was bubbling with happiness, and Laura couldn't stop smiling. Maddie had a good feeling inside her. All her fears of this not working were melting away like butter on a griddle.

When they opened a little while later, she was pleased at how quick and efficient Laura was with serving, and was delighted with her customers' reaction to the coffees. They would need more tables at this rate, since sitting down for a coffee appeared to encourage everyone to have a slice of cake or a cookie. It was a win-win situation, and that was uplifting after the last few weeks of turmoil.

When they both managed a break and a bite to eat mid-afternoon, Maddie took a few recipes out to one of the tables and they went over some of the easier ones. Laura couldn't have been more eager.

"I know you've got enough going on right now, but if you did open a cooking class, you'd have a heap of people wanting to join. You should hear how they rave about your food."

Maddie shook her head. "I've heard some comments, but you've seen what a day looks like for me. When would I get the time?"

"True," Laura agreed with a disappointed sigh.

Maddie opened her mouth once more, although she should have known better. "Actually, I have thought about having a class for my friends. No charge. I think Angel mentioned it to you. It could be a fun night, and it wouldn't be any pressure. If I didn't feel up to it, we could cancel."

Laura's eyes lit up. "Angel did tell me about it. Are you including me?"

"Of course. You're my baker-in-training. You could help."

"Really? How would it work?" Laura was sparkling with pleasure.

"It's not like I've spent a lot of time thinking about it," Maddie laughed. "Everybody brings their own ingredients and some wine. There's plenty of room in the big oven, and we can use my pans and utensils."

"You had me at wine. Count me in."

"It'll have to be after the Girlz and I capture Denise's killer." Shocked at herself, Maddie clapped a hand to her mouth.

Laura grinned. "I'm sorry to break it to you, but it's hardly a secret you and the Girlz are hunting for suspects."

"What do you mean?" Maddie failed miserably at putting together an innocent look.

"The word around town is that you have a list and you're not afraid to use it."

Maddie frowned. "Have you heard anything or know anything else?"

"Everything I know was pulled out of me by Angel. She

didn't want anyone thinking I was involved," Laura said pointedly.

"Right. About that." There was no way she was going to mention all the things on her "Laura list" but she did feel awkward.

Laura shook her head. "Don't give it another thought. I totally get why you would have put me on your list. I might always be a little jealous of you," she grinned

"Why on earth would you say that?"

"Seriously? Look at you, with curves like Marilyn Monroe, the sexiest guy in town hanging on your every word, and loved by everyone. Do you know how that makes us mousey people feel?"

Maddie did an impression of talking, but nothing came out.

"The fact that you have no idea how attractive you are, is even more frustrating," Laura went on. "When I came to town and heard about you, I laughed. Not aloud, of course. People would have thought I was rude, or more likely crazy. I wondered how anyone could have all that going on. Then you came home, and I saw for myself what everyone said was true." She sighed dramatically.

Maddie waved away the compliments. "I don't know who fed you all that, and I've already agreed we can be friends."

Laura laughed hard. "Whatever. I'm not saying these things to flatter you, believe it or not, and I don't think it'll make you big-headed, either way."

The bell over the door rang, thankfully for Maddie, and Angel breezed back in.

"Well, look at the two of you. It makes my little heart jump for joy."

"Glad we can oblige. Doughnut?" asked Maddie.

Angel pouted. "I hate being predictable. Yes, please."

"These have Gran's homemade strawberry jam in them."

"I'm already drooling. Maybe I should take two. I have the Blue Brigade descending this morning."

Laura was horrified. "I don't know how you cope with them. They scare the heck out of me."

"They're not all bad. Some of them are actually very sweet. It's just that when they get together they can get a little mean." She sighed, then grinned. "You know I'm in here so often, maybe I should be asking for a job here too."

Maddie packed up her recipes and headed behind the counter while Laura packaged the doughnuts. "Anytime," Maddie laughed.

"Maybe not. You wouldn't pay me what I make in the salon. Correct?"

Maddie nodded. "Unfortunately, it is, and I need someone who can actually cook."

"But you hired me," Laura reminded her.

"Because you're one butt-kicking barista, and you're going to be a great baker. Angel can't boil water."

Angel nodded. "Sad but true. The awesome thing about our combined professions is that we get to make people feel good inside and out."

"I hadn't thought about it like that, but it's so true," Maddie chuckled.

"Tell Angel about your idea," Laura said excitedly.

"Big mouth." Maddie was only half-joking. Now, she really would have to make it happen. Why she pulled herself in so many directions, she had no idea, but suddenly it seemed right. "As we discussed some time back, and with Laura's encouragement, I'm going to run a class not just for you, but for all the Girlz to learn the basics of cooking. If you're still interested."

"What part of 'heck, yes' do you need to hear twice? I'll be there with bells on."

"As I told Laura, it can't happen until we've solved the murder. You know, the one you've discussed with her?"

Angel looked sheepish. "I asked her about that day, like I asked everyone in town."

"Yeah, about that. It seems like everyone knows what you've been up to," Laura added.

"Well, I have no idea how they would. I was incredibly careful about my questions and who I spoke to."

Laura and Maddie gave her sidelong looks, but Angel presented them with a picture of blamelessness.

"How's Ethan?" she asked cheerfully.

"Here're your doughnuts," Maddie replied.

It was a stalemate.

Chapter Twenty-Five

Later that week as Maddie was replacing the special tea sets in the cabinet at the end of the day, the bell rang and she turned to find Mickey Findlay with an odd look on his face, as if he were disappointed to see her. This was quickly replaced by a wide smile that did not quite reach his eyes.

"Good afternoon, Madeline. I thought I'd pop in personally and invite you to my talk at the community center."

"Good afternoon. Sorry, your talk?"

"Perhaps you've heard about me standing for election."

Just then Laura came through with more crockery and when she saw Mickey she paled. Frightened she was about to drop something, Maddie took them from her.

"Are you okay?"

She nodded, but her eyes stayed on the man who was regarding her with a rather hostile look.

"Laura. Good to see you. I heard you turned down your parents offer to run again for Mayor?"

"I'm sure you are a better candidate," she said coolly.

Maddie wasn't sure what she was witnessing, but she felt more would be said if she wasn't in the room.

"Excuse me, I'll leave you to talk."

"There's nothing to talk about," Laura insisted.

"Except ensuring you and your friends will be voting for me." He gave them a shark-toothed smile

"I'm sure you'll do fine whether we do or not."

The look he gave them was not in the least friendly. "Let's hope so. Good day."

"Are you okay, Laura?"

She was staring at the door fearfully, as if he might reappear. "What? Oh yes, I'm fine."

"You two don't like each other?"

"Not much. How could you tell?"

"Seriously? You could have cut the air with a knife."

Laura grimaced. "I didn't realize it was that obvious, or maybe I'm past caring. He's a friend of my parents and they called last week to see if I would run again. I told them no. Mr. Findlay was behind their idea of having me as mayor in the first place. Like them he thinks I'm a fool."

"You are no fool, and I think we should all do what makes us happy."

"Me too. Being mayor would have made me more than miserable for sure."

"Then I'm glad you said no. For your sake and mine." She winked at her.

Laura smiled, and went back to cleaning up looking markedly better, so Maddie ventured out to do a few errands including collecting the mail, something she'd made sure she did herself since the first envelope.

Each time she opened the post office box, her heart

pounded. Today, she had good reason. Glancing about her, she could see no one looking even remotely suspicious. Everyone appeared to be going about their business as usual, but she couldn't stop the shiver that ran through her body as she pulled the offending envelope out of the box along with the others.

By the time she got back the bakery was shut, unlike the other businesses along the main street. Thomas nodded at her as he pulled a handful of sausages from the front of his window. Angel was putting rollers in Maude Oliver's blue hair, and Mr. Jenkins from the second-hand shop was cataloguing a new shipment of something.

The only one doing something she shouldn't be doing was Maddie. The envelope forced her steps to slow even as she had the urge to run. She unlocked the shop door and went through to the kitchen.

"Gran? Laura?"

No answer. They must have both gone back to the cottage. Taking no chances, she ran up the stairs and went to her bedroom after collecting a pair of gloves and a knife. She threw the mail on her bed, slipped on the gloves, then picked up the envelope by the edges and ran a knife along the seal. Steeling herself, she pulled out the single sheet of paper.

You must be the most stupid person in town. Did you think I wouldn't see or hear about you and your friends asking their pathetic questions? After all that's happened, you really do have a death wish. Or would you rather one of your friends died? Or Gran? Or the Sheriff? Maybe a bigger fire this time? It's time to move on before someone else gets hurt.

Maddie felt sick. Move on? Whoever was sending these

letters knew her and knew she and the Girlz were involved in some detective work. Were they watching her, or all of them? That would imply there was more than one person involved. A gang of killers in Maple Falls sounded absurd, but then so had Denise being murdered.

Life was becoming crazy, and if Maddie didn't have Gran, the shop, and her friends, she would have been in La-La Land herself. What should she do now? Should she go on not telling Ethan, or should she come clean? There was no way she could endanger her friends any longer if they were the targets of such hate.

She would protect them and Gran like a lion if necessary.

She picked up the letter and sniffed it. There was that familiar smell again, a fragrance someone she knew wore. Someone she saw, not often, but enough to think the pungent odor suited them perfectly.

Virginia! She had worn this fragrance every day since she was a teenager. It was odd that Maddie hadn't seen her around lately. Not that she would come into the shop to buy anything, but she'd initially taken to catching people unawares and chastising them for buying Maddie's cakes and pies as they left.

With Laura, who had headed her list of suspects at one time, now cleared of suspicion, Maddie had deliberately not pushed her fellow sleuths into more action. That didn't stop her from thinking about it or looking closely at the few names left on their list.

Suzy was busy at school, Laura at the bakery, and Angel was tied to her salon, but they'd passed on the news that Virginia had been seen skulking around town on the evenings before and after the murder. This was the biggest tip they had, but after the last letter, Maddie had felt the need to follow up on it alone.

Opinionated and rude as Virginia was, Maddie was glad the woman had never been elected mayor. Their poor town could never have coped with such a mean figurehead. A lump in her throat that was caused just by thinking about Denise made her angry at their lack of progress. Things were moving far too slowly, and there had been too many letters threatening not only herself but those she cared about.

The killer had to be caught, and if it was Virginia, nothing would please Maddie more than helping with her capture. With no-one around Maddie took the opportunity to implement her plan. She loaded Honey with a flashlight, gloves, binoculars and a mini Taser she'd purchased online.

That had been awkward when it arrived a few days ago. Doris from the post office had waited patiently for an explanation of the box, her hand lingering on top of it so Maddie would have to snatch it if she wanted to leave anytime soon. Instead she changed the subject.

"I've been meaning to ask you about your tomato sauce recipe. I've heard it's the best in town," she'd said as sincerely as she could muster.

Doris had all but jumped over her counter to explain the recipe and insisted on writing it down. That had taken quite a bit of time, and it wasn't until another customer came in that Maddie had been able to tuck the package under her arm, thank Doris profusely and make her escape. Maybe she was cut out for the detective business after all.

She packed a light jacket, water and a few snacks just in case she was stuck in her car for hours. Then she dressed in black leggings and a black sweater, tied her hair into a tighter braid and practiced a few rolls over the bed and commando crawls along the carpet. It paid to be prepared for every eventuality.

Ethan wouldn't be happy with the stakeout or the Taser, but he might not have to know about it. As safe as it made her feel to have a useful weapon for protection, her stomach hoped she wouldn't need to use it.

After parking down the road from the real estate shop, Maddie unpacked her bag for something to do. Plus, she wanted to read up on using the Taser once more.

It was a rather pretty blue, with two small ugly spikes in the end. Shaped like a gun, it fit neatly in her hand. Granddad Flynn had loved to hunt, and when she was knee-high to a grasshopper, he'd taken her out with him many times. Hunting rabbits or deer might not be quite the same as shooting a person up close, but she could at least say she knew how to fire a gun with reasonable accuracy.

Her initiation had been shooting cans off a fence, just like in the movies, and Granddad said she was a natural. When you had a self-involved mother, hearing any praise was wonderful; hearing it from either of her grandparents was better than licking cookie batter off a beater.

The Taser felt odd in her hand. It was light, for one thing, and it wasn't exactly like a gun. Not that she'd held one of those in years. Not since Granddad passed away. She bit her lip. No sense in getting maudlin. She had too much to think about. For starters, could Virginia be the murderer? As mean as she was, it didn't feel right. Then again, would it feel any different if it was anyone else from Maple Falls?

She unfolded the instructions and looking through them, noted the effective distance and where to aim. Preferably up to 20 feet and just below the chest. The suggestion was to immobilize the assailant, then run for help. Good advice for someone not known for their physical prowess, although it was true that making dough and hefting trays had strengthened her arm muscles, and living in New York City had definitely toughened her up.

She was having a little flex of those muscles as she focused the binoculars when Virginia's front door opened. Her nemesis looked up and down the street, and Maddie slithered down her seat. Although she was confident she wouldn't be noticed, parked as she was between two cars farther down the road, it didn't hurt to take precautions.

Virginia's car was a sleek black Mercedes. It had been the talk of the town when she bought it with the commission from her first sold property, even though it wasn't brand-new. That had been several years ago, and she must have put all her money since then into opening up her own business and buying designer clothes.

It was ridiculously easy to follow her, since the woman drove below the speed limit and indicated a turn well before she needed to. Maddie had never watched her drive before and was astounded. Virginia was a blunt rip-tear-bust kind of person, not this over-careful type. To be truthful, it was a little disappointing that this surveillance malarkey wasn't more exciting.

They drove on out of town into the countryside, which meant it was now pitch-black outside apart from the light cast from their headlights. The farther they drove, the more nervous Maddie became. She hadn't been overly bothered by the darkness while she was living in New York City, where everything was lit up around the clock. Naturally, that had taken some time to get used to, but a place that size with that many lights had given her a certain illusion of safety she'd appreciated.

Finally, Virginia signaled she was turning. Maddie slowed but drove on past the dirt road. When she was a quarter of a mile down the road, she made a U-turn, then turned off her lights. She parked under a large maple tree, hoping it would give her some camouflage. Next, she slipped on her jacket and stuffed its pockets with the mini Taser and flashlight, then crept slowly down the road. Walking for what seemed hours, Maddie could barely make out the driveway and fences on either side, let alone anything else.

She pulled the flashlight out of her pocket but kept it off as she trained her ears on the sounds around her. All she could hear was the rustling of grass and cows shuffling around in the paddock next door. It *was* cows making that noise, wasn't it?

"Why tonight, of all nights, is there no moon?" she whispered, then bit her bottom lip. Nervousness did tend to make a person talkative, but this was so not the time for that.

Out of the darkness loomed a building. It looked like a barn and went back a long way. A faint light could be seen at the far end. Maddie ran in a half-crouch toward it, like she'd seen in the movies, and found a partially opened door. Peering around it, she sucked in a breath.

She could see a variety of tables and machinery as if it were a small factory which hadn't been used in a while. Virginia was in the middle of the large room sitting on a metal chair, her hands tied behind her back. Her face was pinched in pain, and her mouth made a small 'O' when she saw Maddie in the doorway.

Maddie put a finger to her lips and Virginia nodded, then looked away to where a man dressed in black was standing to one side of her but turned away, so Maddie couldn't see his face. He had a baseball bat in one hand, and he rapped Virginia none too lightly on the knees.

She screamed, "What the heck, Ralph?"

"We had a deal for the land. All this messing around with letters is driving me nuts. From now on, we do things my way, or there'll be consequences. Understand?"

"Yes."

He tapped her once more, with the same reaction. "You say yes, but I know you. As soon as I leave, you'll be back to your old tricks. We have one thing to concentrate on. After that's taken care of, you can do what you want with that nosey baker."

Virginia snuck a fearful look at Maddie, which confused her. Was she scared for herself or for Maddie, someone she disliked intensely and whose life she'd been hell-bent on making as miserable as she could? After all these years, Virginia had proven she had Maddie in her sights and still wanted to hurt her, but right now, she was at someone else's mercy.

The knowledge played havoc with Maddie's sensibilities. She could leave Virginia in the hands of this murderer, because surely that's who he was, or she could help her.

Unfortunately for Maddie, her innate sense of right and wrong stepped up to the plate, and she knew she couldn't abandon Virginia. She also knew that Gran would be bitterly disappointed if she didn't at least try to help someone in distress.

Decision made, Maddie crept around the building to see if there was another way in. There was a door conveniently ajar in the corner where the building abutted a smaller one. Maddie wrestled with her pockets. That wouldn't do if she needed the Taser in a hurry. She grasped a weapon in one hand and put the other down her bra, hoping that decision wouldn't hurt her, then slipped through the doorway.

A hand grasped hers and wrestled the flashlight away,

as she was dragged farther inside. She attempted to scream, but another hand was already wrapped around her mouth with a cloth held against her lips and nose. A horrible smell flooded her nostrils as she twisted and turned. He was too strong, and things began to get fuzzy.

Had he killed Virginia? Was she next?

Chapter Twenty-Six

When Maddie tried to open her eyes, they felt like lead. She increased her effort and she had to blink several times before things came into focus. She was still in the building where Virginia had been tied up, the difference being that the room was now deserted apart from herself, and she was the one tied to the chair. Also, both doors were wide open, making the place lighter.

Rope bit into her wrists as she searched the length of it with her fingers. It was a good knot, but one end of the rope was dangling slightly. She traced back again until she found where it had been pulled through. Her fingertips screamed at the abuse as she fought to free that trailing end.

The sound of a car coming closer made her stop. She knew that sound. Her Jeep came through the doors and her teeth clenched as whoever it was behind the wheel pulled Honey up beside her and slammed the car into park with no care whatsoever. The driver climbed out, slammed the door shut, and came close. So close that she could see his coal-colored eyes as he studied her. The man at the funeral,

Maddie realized. Virginia had called him Ralph. If it was the same man, was he Ralph Willis—Mickey Findlay's nephew?

"Good, you're awake. How's the head?"

The questions were asked in the same nasal voice she recognized from earlier, so she now knew his name. His question held no real concern, but it was probably prudent to play along.

"Now you mention it, not too good. Was that chloroform?"

"You know your drugs. Or was it a lucky guess?" he sneered. "Shame you aren't so good at other guesses."

He was about as pleasant as a rattlesnake, and his breath could turn milk sour.

"Do you mean about knowing you're a murderer, or Virginia being your accomplice?"

He grinned, his glee far worse than the sneer. Added to that, his creased clothing, grubby nails and black eyes made him look positively feral.

"I didn't say I murdered anyone, did I? I was referring to your sleuthing abilities. Or lack of them. Following Virginia wasn't your best idea, was it?"

Things were falling into place, and Maddie had to admit she was a prize fool. "I guess Virginia led me here on purpose. That was all part of your plan."

"You figured it out at last. You're not bad-looking, you know? It's a shame you're a little slow."

Maddie held back her temper. She had the feeling it would only make this man happier to see her lose control, so she ignored the bait. "Was Virginia even tied up?"

"Of course she was." He laughed, a creepy sound. "For some reason, she didn't like that part of it, but I like to keep some things real." He ran a dirty fingernail down Maddie's cheek.

She shuddered, despite trying not to. "You have a strange idea of what's real and how to set your priorities."

"Being a local star, you would think so. But your scholarship didn't work out like you expected, did it?"

She looked away, but he dragged her chin back so she was facing him.

"I know what I want, and I find a way to get it. Most people are like that. Even you. Taking money from an old lady to get your shop makes us more alike than you'd think." He shrugged as he walked around her, and Maddie wanted to slap that sickly grin off his face.

"I beg to differ. Most people won't kill to get what they want."

"Ha! Maybe not in dear sweet Maple Falls, but I figure it's different in New York City, isn't it? I can't imagine why you'd come back to this one-horse town after you escaped its clutches."

"Because it's a great place to live if people like you would let us be."

"You have a lot to say for somebody in your position. I think you've done as much as any one person could to ensure you're the next on my list. Ironic since I was never on one of yours, right?"

With a conviction she didn't feel in the slightest, Maddie stuck out her chin as she continued to fumble with the rope behind her. "I figure you've already made up your mind to kill me. I know too much."

"Wow. You're determined not to make it out of here alive, aren't you? Keep talking, lady, and we can start the countdown right away, if that suits you better."

She froze for a minute, then decided that at least if he

was talking, he wasn't killing her. "You wanted Denise to sell you back the land your father donated. Is that right?"

He gave her an appraising glance, then shrugged. "Maybe you're not quite as stupid as you seem."

She should be concentrating on not aggravating him, and on the frayed end of rope she'd found, but his manner was so darn infuriating, and he was just plain rude. "If I'm stupid, it's because I've been chasing stupid people doing stupid things. Like the notes you had Virginia send."

He slapped her. Her head whipped back so hard, she thought it might leave her neck. She touched the corner of her mouth with her tongue, tasting the metallic tang of blood.

Apparently, no one liked to be called stupid. *Note to self: try to keep mouth shut in front of killer when he's angry.*

"Guess again," he smirked.

Her brain offered her several solutions. None of them made much sense, but she had to say something.

"Virginia sent the notes to make sure I'd stay out of it and wouldn't involve the police."

"Sure, she wants to get her percentage for selling the land, but you're missing the most obvious reason."

He pulled on her braid, and her head snapped back again. Ralph had better kill her, because if he didn't, she'd make him pay for every ounce of pain he was inflicting. He was enjoying playing with her emotions, so she put more effort into keeping her face blank.

"She was annoyed at Denise for winning the election?"

"That too. And?"

"I give up."

He sighed and leaned over her to say what he'd obviously been dying to. "She's love-struck, and you're in the way, just like Denise was."

As much as she didn't want to show him how much that affected her, she could feel her eyes widening, and her head throbbed even more than it had been. To make matters worse, with his face in hers, this horrible man's breath was gag-worthy.

Were Virginia's feelings for Ethan so strong she would help kill for them? How was it possible that Ethan had all these adoring women fighting over him? Maybe that was why she was so reluctant to encourage him. Fighting for a man simply wasn't in her nature. Dying for one, even less so. The whole business was all too much.

"You're not going to sleep, are you?"

She hadn't realized her eyes were closed. "I might. Now I know what this is all about, there doesn't seem much point to the conversation. You can set Virginia's mind at ease when you explain that she's totally mistaken about us being rivals."

"I'd rather not listen to your ramblings, either, and I'll let you give her that news. Let's see if you can convince her better than you did me. Tell you what, I'll wake you before lover boy gets here."

"Ethan?" Her eyes shot open.

"Who else? One of Virginia's notes went under his door an hour ago. I expect him to be here very soon."

Dawn was inching up the smeared windows. Her head was still throbbing, making thinking an issue, but she needed a plan. If Ethan was coming here, Ralph and Virginia hoped to kill two birds with one shot. Or something like that.

"What if he brings his deputies?" she blurted, semi-hopeful, but not meaning to give this creep any help.

He just laughed. "Ha! He's as dumb as you are. He'll come alone."

"Not unarmed," she taunted.

"What do you care, if he's not your lover? Anyway, it won't make a difference, since his car is missing brakes," he said, then began to chew on a hangnail as calmly as if he'd said Ethan would be taking a Sunday drive.

"You sabotaged his brakes?" She could barely spit out the words.

He shrugged. "It's a backup, in case he tries to get away. It might not come to that, but don't hold your breath."

"I hope he does get away," she muttered, not sure what Ethan was getting away from.

"I'm sure you do, but as you're not interested in him, what do you care?" He taunted.

"Because he's a person, and a friend."

She must have been asleep—make that unconscious—for several hours if Ralph had time to tamper with Ethan's brakes and get back here. Unless Virginia managed to do so before or after she'd delivered the note? Knowing how particular Virginia was about keeping her fake nails in perfect order, Maddie doubted it. And if she was in love with Ethan, she couldn't do that to him. Could she?

"Does Virginia know about the brakes?"

"Are you stupid? Oh, no need for you to answer. That skinny shrew would probably kill me instead if she had any idea."

He actually laughed in a gleeful way, as if he'd relish the challenge.

It was total daylight now, and the shadows were receding inside the building. Maddie felt sick. How could she possibly stop this from playing out the way Ralph intended?

"Please, let Ethan figure this out," she whispered to herself.

If only she'd told Ethan about the other notes. The two of them might have stood a chance together.

The nerve of this horrible man to go to the funeral, bump into her and casually place a note in her bag. It showed what kind of man he was. And what he was capable of—Denise's death and the fire. The only thing Maddie was glad of was that she hadn't involved her friends in last night's plans.

The bigger picture here was how far Ralph would go to get the land, and what more would Virginia do to get Ethan. Which begged the question—how deeply was Virginia into this? Was she actually a co-murderer? If she was, surely she wouldn't want Ethan to come here?

Mean and *spiteful* were words that sprang to mind, but murder seemed a step too far. Before today, at least.

Chapter Twenty-Seven

Maddie continued to struggle with the end of the rope, but it wasn't budging. She had to come up with another plan. *Think, Maddie.* Seconds later it hit her.

"Excuse me," she called out to the creepmeister, who was sitting in Honey playing with the radio channels, getting his dirty mitts all over the place.

"Shut up. I'm busy," he growled over the static.

The news seemed to be what he was most interested in. No doubt he was looking for anything that revolved around his accomplice or victims. He had turned the volume down, so she had no idea if he was succeeding or not, and she didn't give a flying fig at this moment.

"I need the bathroom. Right now."

"Hold it," he growled again.

She groaned for effect. "I'm afraid that's not possible."

He glared at her over the top of the steering wheel, and she grimaced. He slapped his hands on the wheel, then got out to huff and stomp his way across to her, shoving her keys into his pants pocket. After pulling her roughly from the chair, he frog-marched her to the restrooms in the corner.

Her legs protested from sitting so long, and the pins and needles actually brought tears to her eyes.

"You've got two minutes, so make it fast." He yanked open the door, then none-too-gently shoved her through and into a cubicle. "The time starts now." He glared menacingly at her.

Her mouth dropped open, and she blinked a couple of times. "Are you kidding me?"

Grinning, he folded his arms. "I won't look. Promise."

"Even if I believed that, how the heck can I manage if my hands are tied?" Maddie scoffed.

She thought he would refuse, or worse, offer to help, but he shrugged as he undid her hands. "Happy now?"

"I will be if you turn your back."

"You try anything and you'll be sorry." The glint in his eyes dared her to do exactly that. When she waited docilely, he turned reluctantly around and proceeded to check his phone.

Faster than she'd ever moved in her life, Maddie pulled the Taser from her bra thankful he hadn't searched for more than her keys, and sent him sprawling in a heap between the sink and the door. He twitched and made an odd sound in his throat. Hopefully, she hadn't done him any permanent damage.

Pushing the odd thought to the back of her mind so she could concentrate on the possibility of Virginia getting back anytime, she tied his hands with the rope he'd used on her.

She heard a faint noise, and her skin prickled. Standing on the toilet to peer through the bars on the windows she could see a large turning area, but no cars and no people.

What, or whoever, was out there might be headed this way. Should she stay quiet or make a run for it?

She had to at least try to escape. Grabbing the bars she pulled as hard as she could. They were solid, and there wasn't a hope in making them budge even an inch. Jumping down she put her hands under Ralph's arms, straining to pull him away from the door. For a small man he was darn heavy.

Then the door handle eased downwards, making her gasp. To her relief, the body still half in front of it made an effective doorstop. Which was both good and bad, since the only way out was through that door.

She gave Ralph a nudge with her shoe to make sure he would pose no threat. He groaned, which encouraged more purposeful grunts from the other side of the door, which, to her horror, had opened fractionally. Fingers gripped the edge as they pushed again. It moved a little more. There was no choice. Maddie braced herself to use the Taser on another person—until she heard his voice.

"Maddie? Is that you?"

"Ethan? Thank Goodness! Hang on a second."

She grabbed the twitching body under the arms and moved it an inch at a time until Ethan could squeeze through.

"Are you okay?" he looked her up and down as if he needed to make sure.

She waved away his concern. "He did it, Ethan. He's the murderer," she said, pointing at the man. "I believe it's Ralph Willis. Virginia is in on it too. I followed her here."

He nodded as bent over the prone body and took the man's pulse. "I know. We've been following Ralph for days."

She gaped at him. "What? Why didn't you tell me?"

He frowned. "Hmm. I don't know. Why didn't you tell me about the other letters?"

She flinched at his quiet anger but was confused. "Who told you about them?"

Finally, he looked up at her. "That's not really the point, is it?"

Uncomfortable with his censoring look, she focused on Ralph. "Is the point that we have the killer?" she asked hopefully.

Ethan let out an exasperated sigh. "Let's leave it at that for now, but you and I will be having a serious talk about lying to me and using a Taser. Amongst other things."

She nodded, feeling like a small child about to be grounded. With the wail of sirens in the distance, it looked like her sleuthing days were done.

Ethan manhandled the small man out of the bathroom and into the factory, where he swapped the rope for handcuffs. By that time, Ralph was awake and glaring at them.

"You have no idea what you're doing, or who you're messing with."

Ethan pushed him down into the chair both Maddie and Virginia had vacated. Then he used his best sheriff's voice, which seemed more than enough to bring a person into line.

"I know your name is Ralph Willis, and I know you had no idea what you were doing when you came back to our town. A man like you sticks out like a sore thumb. A man like you is neither wanted nor needed. I think you'll find your next stop much more welcoming."

Ralph spat on the floor. "This town is full of ignorant, small-minded people. You can keep it. I'll be glad to be out of here. Anywhere is preferable to this."

"Then it looks like everyone's a winner. So glad we could help you out."

Maddie needed some air. Ethan followed her to the doorway as two patrol cars pulled up in a screech of brakes, dirt and stones flying from underneath their tires. Officers jumped out, guns at the ready, leaning over hoods and car doors just like they did in the movies. Maddie's legs stopped moving, but her head swiveled back and forth like a clown head at a fair–the kind you put balls in the open mouth.

Ethan walked out into the sunshine with his palms out. "You can stand down. It's all under control, boys. The mayor's alleged murderer is inside."

When he made to walk back into the barn, Maddie touched his arm. "I guess I should say thanks."

"You guess?" Exasperation was written all over his face.

"I'm still annoyed you were following him without telling me. He said he cut your brakes. You might have gotten hurt."

He ran his hands through his hair, making it stand up in random spots. "Oh, Maddie. What am I going to do with you? I'm the sheriff. It's my job to deal with dangerous situations."

She frowned. "Maybe you should look into being a carpenter. You're very good at it."

His mouth twitched. "Thanks, but I could say the same for you with baking."

"I can assure you I'll be happy to get back to my baking."

"What about being a super-sleuth?"

She shrugged. "Oh, no. This was a one-time thing. It's too much work, and to be honest I don't like the dark that much."

His eyes twinkled. "Do you promise?"

She was about to do just that when she thought of all the information she and her friends had gathered over the course of the investigation. Ethan saw her hesitation and slapped his thigh with his hand.

"I knew it!"

"No, it's not what you think. This isn't finished yet. Why Denise got killed doesn't explain the letters and my involvement. Virginia was also involved."

"The chicken and the egg."

"Pardon me?"

"I'm thinking the letters were a direct response to you sticking your nose into Ralph's plans."

"But the letters said I had to stay away from you."

"Makes sense, since I'm the sheriff, and you were finding clues left, right, and center."

She flushed with pleasure. "I don't think that's all there is to it, but you have to admit we did a good job."

He shook his head. "I admit you found out some interesting things, like this business with the typewriter, but you should have come to me, not your friends."

"Ethan, I deferred once before to a man, and lost my independence. I'm never doing that again," she said defensively.

His eyes widened. "You're lumping me in with your ex?"

She knocked a stone with the tip of her shoe. "Maybe I am, because of our history. I realize that's not fair and I should have shown you the letters. I'm stubborn, there's no denying it, but I was trying to protect you. Just like you've been trying to protect me through all of this. For me the threats against you and Gran were too real and too awful to think about."

"I've been over that. It's my job to do the protecting, and

no, I'm not likely to give it up anytime soon, if that's what you're thinking. Let's get going."

She sighed, as they walked to his car. It was exactly what she was thinking, along with other burning questions. Waiting until they were headed back to town, she half turned to him. "Did you have a thing with Denise? And Virginia? She was involved with the Ralph thing, you know. She delivered the letters at the very least."

It looked like he wasn't going to answer, then he shrugged. "I've never had anything but—let's call it a wary respect for Virginia. Her company flourished despite her attempts to alienate the whole town. As for Denise, yes, I did. For a few months, some time ago. We thought it was a secret, but apparently neither of us was good at that sort of deception."

"Good enough to fool me."

Ethan let out a long sigh. "No one intended to fool you. As I recall, you left both me and the town, not the other way around."

"I didn't go on a whim. We agreed to call a halt to our relationship, since I'd be gone for a few years. I had no intention of staying away forever. Maybe you weren't happy about it, but we did agree. Remember?"

"I'm pretty sure I had no choice."

"Then you should have said something a whole lot earlier than you did."

He held a hand up. "You're right. Let's not get into that again."

She nodded, but wasn't finished with the rest. "So, why was it a secret about you and Denise?"

"She was running for mayor. We wanted to keep it quiet because we knew it wasn't a big deal to either of us, but the town might not have been happy about the prospective mayor and the sheriff being an item. It was two lonely people enjoying each other's company. No harm. No foul. Is that so wrong?"

"Not wrong, only we're all in the same circle of friends. It would have been nice to know."

"Nice? How so? All it would have meant was you could judge us, like the rest of the town. Like you're doing now. Can't you be glad that we had a little happiness when we were both feeling alone? Denise had a tough time fitting into a mayor's shoes, and I had the promotion weighing me down. We both had a lot to learn, and every eye in town was on both of us. Surely, you understand how that feels."

He was referring to the guilt she felt about throwing away her career in business development. Now she was working for herself and knew she was doing a good job, the guilt had retreated, and she was being treated as if she had never made that mistake. She hadn't considered Ethan struggled with his own choices.

"I'd have thought you'd be happy to have the job you love."

"I am, but it's been strained going from deputy to sheriff. In a small town where everyone knows you and wants you to treat them as a friend, when it comes to the law, that only makes things more difficult." He straightened. "I'm not complaining, and I don't want to make excuses for Denise and me. You weren't here. You couldn't know or see how it was. It was nobody's business but ours, and I seem to remember you'd found someone else too."

She flinched at the truth of his words. "Therefore I have no right to comment?"

"What do you think?"

She knew she'd overreacted, but it had proven hard to get the image of her friend and her ex-boyfriend together out of her head. Any awkwardness that might have marred their relationship would never happen now Denise was gone, and that made her sad. She was sure she would have accepted them eventually, especially since there was no chance she and Ethan would be anything more than friends.

He pulled into the station parking lot. "Anything else before we go in, pink panther?"

"I'm truly sorry, Ethan."

He must have seen she meant it, because he gave her a relieved smile. "Me too."

"Can we start again?"

"As friends?"

"Always."

He pulled her into a hug and kissed her forehead. His arms around her, and the feeling of safety they provided, reminded her that a friend was worth so much more than anything else.

In fact, it was pretty darn priceless.

Chapter Twenty-Eight

The station had become weirdly familiar. Ethan left her in the waiting room while he took an urgent call. Maddie knew the drill and dreaded the interrogation, but this time, she was in for a surprise. Deputy Jacobs came down the hall full of concern when he saw her. It certainly made a nice change from his previous attitude.

"Can I get you some ice for your cheek, Ms. Flynn?"

She touched the side of her face where Ralph had slapped her, and flinched. With all the drama she'd forgotten about it. Now the pain came back with a vengeance. There would most likely be a bruise tomorrow if there wasn't one already. She was glad there was no mirror, because she felt dirty and a mess. Her hair had escaped the braid in several places, what little makeup she was wearing must be ruined by the treatment she'd been subjected to, and her clothes were covered in dust and grime.

"There's no need. I'll take care of it when I get home. Thanks, Deputy."

"Robert, or Rob," he said with a smile.

There had to be a first time for everything, and Maddie

wasn't immune to how a small thing could change the way you looked or felt about a person. Maybe Rob wasn't the uptight stickler she'd thought he was.

"I hear you helped capture Ralph Willis. That was very brave of you."

"Thanks, Rob." She peered around him.

"Mr. Willis has already been taken down to the cells, so you don't need to worry. You're safe here."

That was a relief. "Is Ethan coming back?"

"He said he would as soon as he's done with the call."

Maddie felt exhaustion creep through her. If Ethan didn't hurry, she was might just stretch out on the chairs.

Before that could eventuate, the door opened, and in walked Angel and Laura, with Virginia between them. Maddie would surely have fallen over if she hadn't been sitting. At the same moment, Ethan strode purposefully down the hall from the opposite direction.

If she was a mess, Virginia was worse. This was something Maddie had never seen. The weird thing was that her enemy looked like she'd given in as well as giving up.

"Can someone please tell me what's going on? My mind isn't capable of processing this right now." Her finger traced a circle of the group in the air.

Angel was close to, but not touching Virginia, and didn't seem angry or perturbed by it.

"Virginia came to tell us about Ethan's car being tampered with. She was scared for him. We called him, then hid Virginia until he told us to come to the station."

Her tone implied she was mighty annoyed, but the foot tapping said way more. And it was Maddie who appeared to be the problem, not Virginia.

Maddie sighed. "I meant to call you after I followed

Virginia and saw where she was going. It escalated so fast I didn't have time."

"Time enough to pack Honey with supplies for a stake-out." The toe-tapping reached a crescendo.

"I was being prepared."

"Preparing to go behind everyone's backs is what you were doing, and you know it."

Maddie appreciated it was useless to deny the truth. "Will it help if I say I'm sorry?"

"Maybe. Just not right now," Angel fumed.

Maddie turned to Ethan, who was wearing a slightly amused expression. Was he enjoying her discomfort with everyone being upset at her? And what was up with the way they were all treating Virginia, who was surely in this mess up to her thinly plucked eyebrows?

"Come on through, ladies. We have some things to discuss." He pointed down the corridor.

"Wait for me."

Gran came down the hall with Deputy Jacobs. She threw her arms around Maddie, making her wince as Gran squeezed for all she was worth.

"Thank goodness you're safe."

Ethan coughed. "If we're all here? Come into my office."

He ushered them inside and pulled up five chairs before taking his seat behind a large oak desk. Maddie was on one end, and Virginia sat in between Angel and Laura. Angel patted the woman's hand, and Maddie cringed at the gesture.

"I'm so confused by the attitude in this room. Isn't she involved in Denise's murder?" She nodded at Virginia. "I mean she was the one that lured me to that place tonight!"

Angel frowned. "Shush, Maddie. Just listen for a change."

Maddie had just been told off by her best friend while Virginia, the cause of all her problems, calmly sat staring ahead. This was a nightmare.

"She's agreed to tell us everything without the aid of a lawyer, which she's waived the right to, and I think we should hear it together. Go ahead when you're ready," Ethan encouraged.

Virginia clasped her hands, still staring into a distance only she could see.

"When Ralph came to me offering financial backing for the election, I turned him down flat. I didn't want to be responsible for Maple Falls in any way, shape or form. I thought that was the end of it. Then my mom got sick. Very sick. She had no insurance, and the medical bills piled up. I managed for a while, but I couldn't look after her and work full-time. Then she needed hospitalization."

She lowered her head, but not before Maddie had seen tears rolling down her cheeks. Ethan got up and poured a glass of water from the cooler in the corner and placed it gently in Virginia's hands.

She took a few sips, then a deep breath. "Ralph turned up at the right moment, which was clearly not a coincidence. I was desperate. He offered to pay mom's bills if I would run for mayor, and once I took office, I would allow him to buy back his father's lands. I got into the race late, and I knew what people thought of me. It wasn't going to be easy, but I did the best I could. Then the box with the altered forms turned up. Ralph was furious that it was found. He accused me of sabotaging the election. I couldn't prove my innocence, so he threatened my mom again. This time, all I had to do was take a few letters and slip them into the mailbox."

"You wrote those notes, threatening Gran?" Maddie snapped. "How could you when you'd been through that with your mom?"

Virginia glared at her. "I didn't write them. Besides, wouldn't you do anything you could to protect Gran?"

Seeing her point, while not liking the way it was made, Maddie merely nodded. Was it Ralph or Mickey who wrote them?

"I was as shocked as everyone when Denise was murdered, and when your bakery caught fire I knew Ralph had probably done both. I knew, Ralph's aim was to get the land, but I didn't know how far he was prepared to go to achieve it."

Virginia unwound the scarf from her neck. Underneath it, a large cut was dotted with dried blood.

"He could see I'd had enough, and he said that even if I didn't value my own life, he knew I wasn't so blasé about my mom's. After the letters, I said I wanted out, that I'd sell my business and repay every cent. His answer was that he could prove I sent the notes. He'd taken pictures of me mailing them. He also said my debt would be cancelled if I did one last thing. All I had to do was get you to the barn."

"He could have killed me, Virginia."

"I know. And I also knew he was never going to let me walk away, no matter what he said. That's why I contacted Angel and told her where you were."

"Why Angel?"

"She's the nicest out of you all, and even though it would take some time to get her to see I was telling the truth, I knew she'd listen and would get Ethan to do the same. I hoped there would be enough time, and luckily, there was."

Maddie wanted to be outraged, but how could she be? It was true. There was no love lost between any of them and Virginia, but Angel would be the one to give a person a second or third chance.

Something else was nagging at her. "When you said it, I assumed you meant you went to see Angel after you put the note under Ethan's door, and after you had left the factory. But that's not right, is it?"

"No. I went to see them earlier."

Maddie turned to Angel. "That means you all knew about Virginia luring me into danger, but you let me go anyway?"

Angel's look softened. "We did. Ethan assured us it was the only way to catch Ralph in the act. We agonized over it, so don't think it was easy to make the call, but in the end, I knew you would have agreed to go, but if we told you, you wouldn't have acted as surprised as you should."

"I don't like that you took the choice away from me."

"We understand that, but Ethan was with you all the way," Laura interjected.

"He wasn't there when I was chloroformed, or when I was slapped. He wasn't there when I was tied up or trapped in the bathroom with a killer."

Gran made a disgusted noise, Laura paled, as did Angel. Ethan had the good grace to look uncomfortable.

"I couldn't find your car, and the factory isn't visible from the road. I thought I knew where Virginia was talking about, but the sign must have been taken down since the last time I was out that way."

Virginia sat forward. "I offered to go with you. It's not my fault you can't read a map."

"I could have told you that," Maddie almost laughed. It may have been a bit of hysteria.

Ethan ignored her. "Yes, you did offer Virginia, but we couldn't know if there were any other people involved. We still don't know for sure. Hopefully, Ralph will spill the beans."

"Hopefully?" Maddie asked.

"Ralph is a piece of work, I wouldn't be surprised if his uncle hangs him out to dry."

Maddie was wiping her face with her sleeve, feeling grit in every pore, and she stilled.

"His uncle?" Laura asked quietly.

"It's conjecture, but, yes. Mickey Findlay." Ethan answered.

"Wow. This is complicated," she said.

"Ralph Willis's father was old man Willis. His mother was Cora Findlay," added Gran, who prided herself on knowing everyone in town. "Cora ran away many years ago with her son. Her parents left the house to Mickey, but Cora got all the money and they had a great deal, so I assume she lived quite well."

"She was a wealthy woman for sure but kept a very low profile for some reason." Ethan kept his voice slow and steady. "On her death she left all her land to Mr. Willis who never got over his heart break over losing his family. He didn't want it, so donated all the land we use for our festivals and markets to the town. Although, neither of them cared about money, it seems like their son is cut from a different mold."

"So, Ralph finds out who he's related to and comes to town to get his land only to find it's been given away?" Maddie asked.

"Exactly. We know he contacted Mickey Findlay and

that's when it gets ugly. Although, we have no proof of his involvement other that the family tie."

The last piece of the puzzle slipped into place, but Maddie had to tie up all loose ends. "So, where does this leave things with Virginia. Does she walk away scot-free?"

"That's up to the court."

"If I go to jail," Virginia whispered, "what happens to my mother?"

Maddie leaned around Angel. "You should have thought about that. She's going to be hurt either way now. If I had a mother as sweet as yours, I wouldn't want that. All you had to do was ask for help instead of being so mean all the time."

"Leave it," Angel said. "This isn't the time."

Virginia stood, back straight, face pale but determined. "I deserve to go to jail, but don't think you know enough about me which gives you the right to judge my relationship with my mom. Ethan, can I go to another room or to my cell?" Her bottom lip wobbled.

"Sure." Ethan took her out of the room and back down the hall.

Maddie turned to the friends who had lied to her. They were watching her closely too, trying to gauge her reaction. Maybe "lie" was too harsh a word for what had happened. They'd kept her in the dark, which was no different from what she had done to them.

Ethan was still absent, which gave her the opportunity to ask one more burning question.

"I'd like to know whether Virginia would have done the same thing to me if she hadn't been in love with Ethan and seen me as a threat."

"What?" Angel was all but off her chair as she swiveled around in shock.

"Don't tell me I actually know something you two don't?"

"Ethan and Virginia? Impossible."

Ethan chose that moment to return, and Angel flushed at being overheard.

"Don't start that rumor again. There's never been anything between us," he said firmly to all of them, but more so to Maddie.

"Maybe not from your end, but you have to know she's in love with you. It's so obvious. She can't tear her eyes away from you. Plus, she did threaten me outside the bakery, when she told me to stay away from you."

Ethan didn't answer, but he looked mighty uncomfortable.

"I didn't notice anything." Angel's eyes were wide with shock.

"I always knew how she felt," Laura sighed deeply.

Maddie wouldn't embarrass Laura by pointing out that she would know how Virginia felt more than anyone else, since she was also smitten with the sheriff. She rubbed her wrists. "Can I go home?"

Ethan nodded. "Let the Girlz drive you after you sign the statement I've prepared. They can do theirs tomorrow and pick up your car. It'll be safe here tonight."

Poor Honey, left stranded all over the county instead of tucked up in the garage. Maddie didn't have the strength to argue.

Chapter Twenty-Nine

The trial proved to be enlightening in many ways. Most of the town drove over the hills to Destiny to see the killer brought to justice, since there was no court in Maple Falls.

On the day Virginia was due to begin testifying, Maddie had closed the shop and drove over with Angel, Suzy and Laura. Although, the three of them were still a little cool over her ditching them to catch Ralph. Especially Angel.

Virginia sat in the witness box wearing a simple business suit and no makeup, looking haggard as she told her story. Everything she'd said in the room at the station was repeated, with the addition of a few more personal touches that gnawed at Maddie's perception of the mean girl who'd turned into a mean woman.

It seemed Virginia had a violent upbringing at the hands of her father, and when Denise, her best friend at the time, had found out and wanted to tell someone, that was when they had their falling out. She was barely fourteen.

Virginia had been too scared to do anything until a few months later, when, after another beating, she ran her father off with a shotgun. He'd threatened to return, and she had lived with that fear all this time, keeping people at bay the only way she knew how, with a show of bravado and fierceness.

"I wanted to handle the sale of the land. I admit that freely. It was for the reasons I've stated and nothing more. I did leave the letters, which were given to me by Ralph Willis, but had no idea of the content. When I realized what Ralph truly intended with regards to Madeline Flynn and Ethan Tanner, I alerted the Sheriff, offering to help them if they could protect my mother." She took a drink of water with a shaky hand. "I didn't have anything to do with killing the mayor. We weren't friends, but I was okay with that, and so was she."

The last part was the lead in the newspaper the next day.

Ralph did himself no favors with his snarling and threatening looks, mainly directed at Maddie.

It was as clear as seafood bisque that there was a bigger fish than Ralph involved, but the creep wouldn't admit to it. The lawyers went around in circles for far too long.

Then it was Ethan's turn to testify. In full uniform, he stepped into the witness stand. He was sworn in and the prosecutor began asking him questions revolving around his ability to testify and what he had witnessed. It was stuff they all knew until the prosecutor handed Ethan a book.

"What the sheriff holds is our late mayor's diary. Every event she went to over the last year is noted in this, and there are several more like it. There are also the day-to-day thoughts of a woman whose every intention was doing right by her town."

There were many gasps and the scraping of seats as if

there was a way to get closer to hear this latest turn of events.

"The mayor had several visitors in the week leading up to her death, and when we put the list next to the list of the people who felt ill at that time, we can see a direct correlation with the people who complained of stomach problems. We already know that the mayor had an admirer who left her gifts of cupcakes, supposedly from Maple Lane Bakeries, but we also know that isn't the case. Please tell us what happened Sheriff."

Ethan looked across to where Ralph was sitting next to his lawyer whispering and he sat straighter. "During the course of this investigation, several letters of a threatening nature were sent to Madeline Flynn. The last one, and my car, have the accused's fingerprints on them."

Maddie held her breath as Ethan answered questions about her being kidnapped. The prosecutor showed the jury photos of her bruised face, the factory, and Ralph's hotel room, where all the necessary implements for kidnapping and car tampering were found.

It was a long day and it was only the first of several as the trial progressed.

Mickey Findlay was eventually put on the witness stand, his smug attitude not winning him any friends.

"I have no clue what my Nephew, who I haven't seen since he was a baby, has been up to. I did want to purchase the land that was my birthright. When I was told no, I left it at that. If my nephew felt the need to return it to the family, that has nothing to do with me."

Maddie didn't believe him for a second and was on the edge of her seat when the typewriter was brought out. The defense attorney who had been privy to the diary and the knowledge of the typewriter was quick to point out that it was used by Mickey's secretary, but Anna Ramsey had been out of town when the last letter had been sent, and she stated that it was for show and she only used a computer.

Unfortunately, it couldn't be proved that it wasn't written before by her, Ralph or someone else and Ralph wasn't talking. With no other person deemed to be involved and no witnesses to prove otherwise, Mickey Findlay walked away with a swagger.

A few days later, Ralph Willis was found guilty of murdering Denise and a list of other crimes leading up to the murder and afterwards, including the poisoning of several residents. The gallery gasped at the very idea, and Maddie was again reminded that Gran could have died too.

Virginia, apart from posting the letters, had lured Maddie out to the warehouse with the sheriff's agreement. She was given a talking to by the judge about associating with criminals and set free.

Considering everything she heard about her; Maddie's heart softened. How a person was could often be attributed to an awful past. It was clear she would have done almost anything for her mom, but Virginia had no doubt suffered enough.

In need of a way to celebrate, and also commiserate, the Girlz went back to Maddie's with Gran, who insisted they have a drop of brandy in their tea.

"Don't drink it if you don't like it, but I'm in need of a pick-me-up. I still feel bad that I didn't share everything Denise told me. If I had, this might never have happened."

Maddie gave her a hug. "Don't blame yourself. He was a horrible little man who wanted what he couldn't have and was going to stop at nothing to get it. All you did was try to be a good friend and keep a secret. None of us is responsible for Denise's death."

"I'll try." Gran wiped a stray tear and took a big sip of her doctored brew.

Suzy tried to change the subject. "I don't suppose you can use Virginia now to sell the cottage. What will you do, Gran?"

Maddie screwed her nose up at the concoction but drank it anyway. "Actually, we were never going to use her after how rude she was about buying this place. I contacted a few agents from Destiny, and we even made appointments for them to look at the house, but no one showed up."

Angel placed her empty cup on its matching saucer, decorated with a pink rose. "That's not very professional."

Gran got up and poured herself another brandy, minus the tea, much to their astonishment, as she rarely drank. "About that."

Maddie groaned. "Not another secret, Gran?"

Gran looked as guilty as a dog with a stolen bone, and while the others seemed amused, Maddie truly was worried. They'd just finished with one mystery, and she had no idea what to expect from her grandmother. Lover of secrets and confidant to so many—it could be any darn thing. And since when did she need a drink to give her courage?

"I've decided I don't want to sell my house."

Maddie dropped her cup in her saucer. "Why not?"

Gran came back to the table and sat close to her. "You were right. It's my home, and I want to stay here."

"I don't understand. You don't want to go into a retirement community?"

"No."

"Okay, then. How will you manage now you've given me all your savings?"

If anything, Gran looked even guiltier. "I don't actually

need any money. It's true I used all my savings helping you buy the bakery, but I still have your Granddad's family money if I get desperate."

Maddie didn't know a thing about family money, and she didn't care right now. "If you have other money, why did you consider selling the house?"

"In all honesty, I didn't think it would get this far. I wanted to help you, and it seemed like the only way."

"I never wanted you to sell, either, and I can take care of myself."

"I never said you couldn't, but you're so stubborn, you wouldn't have let me buy the bakery outright for you, so I had to think of another way."

"Gran, did you set this whole thing up with the sole purpose of me coming home?"

"I did."

Despite her blush, Gran looked very pleased with herself, and the Girlz were all smothering grins. Maddie frowned at them.

"Don't encourage her, please. That isn't cool, Gran. You can't manipulate people like that."

"It *is* terrible," Gran admitted. "But it worked out okay, don't you think?"

Maddie was exasperated. "Did you have any intention of selling?"

Gran shrugged. "If that was the only way to convince you."

"I'll take that as a no."

"Well, there is a difference, so it wasn't an outright lie."

Maddie shook her head at Gran's deviousness, then she had another realization. "Did you cancel those appointments I made with the other agents?"

Gran folded her arms across her floral apron. "I had to.

We couldn't waste their time, coming all this way for nothing," she said reasonably.

Maddie sighed. "So, the place isn't too big for you?"

"Not now Laura's moved in."

Laura beamed at Gran. "I'd love to stay, too, but only if you let me pay rent. Then you won't have to touch your husband's money."

"See?" Gran said to Maddie. "Things are all working out. Besides, if I can bake beside you every day, I can manage a house. I did it for years, managing a home, working around the farm, baking, and raising you. There's a bit of life left in this old dog yet."

Big Red raised his head at the mention of the D-word, saw it was a false alarm, and curled back onto Maddie's feet.

Gran might be nearly seventy, but she was as sharp as a tack, and she worked as hard as Maddie did. And it was true that she had done all those things, plus, while Maddie was in school, she had cooked for people and made an extra living from it. Funny how she had done it despite not really needing the money.

Maddie sighed and poured another cup of tea, minus the brandy, which she suspected was courage for Gran and a way to make Maddie more amenable to the story that unfolded.

"You're an old rascal."

Gran chuckled. "Now, now, there's no need for name-calling. Are you happy with the bakery and your apartment?"

"I love them both."

"Then my job is done."

Gran clinked her teacup against Maddie's and, with a smug smile, downed the last of her brandy. "Now that I'm back here, I can stop this foolish packing, and you can have plenty of room to entertain and get your cooking class up and running."

By now, the Girlz were laughing too, but they also had tears in their eyes.

Maddie shook her head. "What's wrong with all of you?"

Angel wiped her cheeks with a tissue. "We want someone to love us like that."

Maddie was astonished. Then she looked at her Gran, and a love so strong it was almost overwhelming flowed through her. Tricking Maddie into coming home, pretending she was getting too old, was terrible, and yet so awesome. She had given Maddie what Maddie hadn't been willing to take on her own. Everything, and then some.

Now, this was a perfect day.

Chapter Thirty

The women gathered around Maddie's kitchen counter at the back of the shop. It was huge, large enough for the four of them to have a space each.

"Finally, we can get back to a normal life." Angel sighed, then took a sip of wine.

"Nearly normal. Ethan isn't happy with us," Laura added.

Suzy grinned. "I wouldn't have guessed. He's been grumping all over town at the people who knew things but only told us."

Laura topped up their glasses. "Poor Ethan. I guess he was right—we were playing a dangerous game, even if that wasn't our intention."

Maddie took exception to that. "It was no game to me. I know he was right about a lot of things, but we did do some good."

Gran, who'd come into the room, sniffed as she walked around them. "Big Red and I are going for a walk while you justify your behavior. I'll be glad to get home to the cottage tomorrow and have things back to normal."

"Gran!"

"Don't 'Gran' me. You know you could have gotten yourself killed, Madeline Flynn. If that had been the case, I would have been very angry with you."

Knowing she was serious, Maddie hid a smile. "Like you said, it all worked out in the end."

"No thanks to you four," Gran huffed as she went out the door.

"I can understand how she feels," Angel said so quietly that Maddie thought she had misheard her.

"Hang on a minute. You were all in this with me."

"We were until you went out on your own. Following Virginia could have been the worst decision you'd ever made in your life. Ralph could have killed you outright and not waited until later."

Maddie shuddered. It wasn't as if she hadn't given that some thought afterwards or had some nasty dreams over it. "I'm sorry. It won't happen again."

"It's not funny."

"No, Angel, it's not. And it's not funny how Virginia's childhood made her morph into a person full of hate and do things she knew were wrong."

Angel twirled her glass, staring into the pale liquid. "Loving the same man as another woman can do that. I should know."

"Are you talking about Ethan and Virginia, or you?"

"Both."

"Oh, Angel, your husband was a pig!" Suzy exclaimed.

"True, but just because you know something about someone doesn't mean you can turn the love off. Don't worry," she said in response to their horrified looks. "Brad is someone in my past, and I see him for what he was—and still is. At the time, it wasn't so easy to grasp. That's why I had to start again, working at a job I hated, because he never let me believe I was any better than that."

Laura patted her hand. "A man doesn't have that power unless we give it to him."

"Hindsight is a good thing, but it's always in the future, isn't it?"

Sometimes Angel saw the darkest things with the utmost clarity.

Maddie nodded. "If I had it to do over, I would have told Ethan about the notes. I should have trusted him to keep us all safe, including himself. Hopefully he'll get over being angry with us sometime soon."

Angel finally smiled. "And you can give him a second chance."

"Don't even go there. I think there're enough women in this town who think they're in love with our sheriff, and I'm enjoying being a single woman, hanging out with my single friends." Maddie meant every word, but she was sorry for making Laura so uncomfortable with discussing Ethan this way.

Then her red-haired new friend held out her hand. "Have you got a pen and paper and the phone book?"

Maddie moved to where her pad and pen sat, her curiosity piqued. "What do you need them for?"

"To make the list, of course."

"What list?" Suzy asked.

Laura laughed. "I know how much you love them, so I thought we'd make a list of all the women who've got an eye for Ethan. Then you won't have to wonder anymore."

Maddie scooped a handful of flour out of the container and blew it over Laura while the rest of the women hooted. When her friend leaned over, threatening to do the same, Maddie held up her hands.

"My kitchen, my rules. No food fights."

When they'd calmed down, Suzy raised her glass.

"Let's celebrate with another glass of wine. I feel like we missed celebrating the capture of Denise's killer what with all of the aftermath of our detective work and the trial."

Maddie nodded. "One more glass. Then we bake."

"Yes, o fearless leader."

Maddie went for the bowl of flour again, and Suzy stood behind Laura.

While they sipped, Maddie checked that she had everything. "Okay, let's get into this recipe. We'll read it through once, then you can ask questions. After that, you can follow me step by step."

The women stepped back into their positions behind the counter and began to diligently read while Maddie watched, wondering how hard it would be to get them baking some basics. As soon as they'd finished, Suzy raised her hand as if she were still in school rather than its principal.

"What's the difference between baking powder and baking soda?"

"Good question, Ms. Barnes."

Maddie answered the question in such detail that the other Girlz' eyes began to glaze over.

Suzy yawned. "I'm kind of sorry I asked."

"Okay, then. Let's get started."

Each step needed repeating several times, and what should have taken twenty minutes took over an hour. They were truly bad at this, but what they lacked in technique they made up for it in enthusiasm.

Gran slipped in and gave Maddie a wink before heading upstairs with Big Red, who skirted the noisy group and gave Maddie a disdainful flick of his tail for being unavailable once more.

It took another two hours of tasting their successes and failures with more wine before Maddie could send the other Girlz home. They were so tipsy at that point Maddie had to call Bernie Davis to drive Suzy home while Angel and Laura sang themselves down Plum Place to Gran's.

With a smile on her face, Maddie made her way upstairs, where Big Red was waiting for her. She hefted him into her arms and carried him to her room, her face pressed to his fur.

"What doesn't kill you makes you stronger," she whispered into his neck not really sure if she meant the case or her friends' attempts at baking.

What a night. What a life.

Thanks so much for reading Apple Pie and Arsenic. I hope you enjoyed it!

If you did...

1 Help other people find this book by leaving a review.

2 Sign up for my new release e-mail, so you can find out about the next book as soon as it's available.

3 Come join my private Facebook group.

4 Visit my website for the very best deals.

Keep reading for an excerpt from Bagels and Blackmail.

Bagels and Blackmail

Throwing on an old cardigan and wiping sleep from her eyes, Maddie ran downstairs. Wrenching open the back door she went out into the garden. Lips pursed she whistled softly. Unlike her dream, Big Red hadn't come home in the middle of the night.

With a sigh she headed back upstairs to shower and dress. Except for that dream, Maddie had tossed and turned most of the night, worried about her cat. Perhaps a brisk walk might help her aching head.

Unable to stomach breakfast, she managed a quick cup of tea before heading down Plum Place. It ran along the back of the block of four shops, of which hers was the end one. Two doors down was Angel's Salon.

There were three things about Angel that were a given.

1. She was without a doubt, the prettiest woman in town.

2. Angel loved food (which made her the perfect best friend for a baker).

3. She also loved her sleep.

Like Maddie, she lived above her shop. Unlike Maddie, she woke with just enough time for her hair and make-up before starting work. She worked six days most weeks and they were long days, apart from Saturday when she tried to finish at noon.

In this respect they were also a good match, because most Saturday afternoons and Sunday's they just wanted to relax, and rarely went out at night mid-week. It should bother a couple of twenty-eight year-olds that they had no social life to speak of, but right now they were living their dreams and happy enough with that. It would have been nice if they both had more free time and that might happen when the newest members of staff got more experience.

Maddie stopped at the end of the row, which was the butcher shop, a favorite haunt of Big Red's when he wasn't keeping guard of his own garden at the back of the bakery or visiting Gran.

Half a mile down the end of the street was Gran's cottage where Maddie grew up, after her mom decided that raising a child wasn't the best thing she could do with her life. She had long gotten over the feeling of rejection, because if she was honest it had been a relief. Gran was the best parent/grandparent a person could have and her late Grandad had been just as awesome.

The cottage was and always had been a haven should she or anyone else ever need it. It had also been Big Red's first home. Now, instead of living with Gran, Laura did. Which made perfect sense—Laura needed a place to stay and Gran had company.

Being Saturday the butchers was closed, so it had been a hopeful thought as opposed to anything else that her cat would be hovering around there. She carried on down to Gran's enjoying the fresh air despite her anxiety. She walked most days because after baking, being outside in nature was her favorite place to be. But this was more than a social call.

The door was wide open, the rocking chair empty of Gran or Big Red who usually sat precariously on the back of it whenever he visited. She walked on through the old cottage which had been in the family for three generations.

Gran was in the huge garden with Laura, their heads bent over the same bed of vegetables. Maddie's heart did a little flip, at the red-head so close to the gray, and she allowed herself to acknowledge internally that she was a little envious. This used to be her and Gran out here together, but time wouldn't allow for more than tending to her own small patch at the back of the bakery.

Since they lived in the same house, it was natural the two of them would spend time together, especially when Gran was so caring. In fact, she was the go-to person in Maple Falls for many of the residents and helped them in one way or another.

They were all lucky to have her and it was only right to share the love and it really wasn't so bad. She was able to spend a lot of time with Gran in the kitchen most days, and Laura deserved family time with people who didn't judge her. Having parents who had dictated her whole life until recently, Laura had been a bundle of neurosis when she came to town and put her hat in the ring for the mayoralty.

With Gran in her life and the rest of Maddie's friends to gently push her, she was blossoming into someone who was more self-assured and capable. Heck, even Maddie had found a place in her heart, and that was saying something. The two of them had been at loggerheads from day one, and it had taken Angel, their best friend to get them together. Check for repetition.

Maddie shuddered. She would not think about the death of Denise on this beautiful fall day.

Laura looked up and smiled. The sun glinted off her vibrant red hair and Maddie couldn't help noticing that being happy made her so much more attractive.

"Did you have a relaxing morning, Maddie?"

"I did, thanks. Doesn't it make a difference not getting up at five?"

"It sure does. Gran and I had a lazy morning and haven't long had breakfast, so we thought we'd better do something the day's gone."

"I'm glad both of you managed a bit more rest and the good news is, I've decided to hire a young man called Luke Chisholm, which should make things easier on all of us."

"I wasn't really complaining." Laura's smile was replaced by worry.

Maddie hated that Laura was still so insecure. "I know, but I feel bad that you two have to work so hard for my dream."

Gran brushed dirt from her gloves and tutted. "Don't talk silly, child. We wouldn't do it if we didn't want to."

Laura nodded. "And, you know I'm loving every minute of it. The baking especially."

"All right, I won't slump into depression then."

They all laughed until Maddie remembered her main reason for being there.

"Did either of you happen to see Big Red this morning?"

Gran's smile vanished. She took off her gardening gloves and put them on top of a basket where an array of vegetables lay. "Not since yesterday. That cat has a mind of his own, he could be anywhere."

She was trying to put a positive slant on it but Maddie could see she wasn't as convinced as she sounded. Gran was good friends with Mr. Clayton and no doubt they had discussed more missing pets than just his Sissy.

"I know he likes to wander, but it's not like him to miss breakfast. Perhaps he was annoyed I slept in and he's gone to find his own." She said it as much for herself as for the other two.

"Like a bird?" Laura asked.

Gran and Maddie snorted. Not only did they look alike, or had done at the same age, but they had the same sense of humor.

"Big Red would never expend the energy to catch anything. I don't think he could get his butt off the ground for a start, and actually, he's just plain lazy. He'd rather go sit on someone's doorstep until they cave in and feed him. He's not fussy either. A piece of meat or a croissant is all the same to him." Gran wiped the corner of her eye.

"He certainly is a big cat." Laura admitted warily, not always appreciating their teasing.

Maddie smiled. "To be honest, I believe he thinks he's a dog."

"That makes sense, since he's certainly big enough to be one." Gran tucked her arm through Maddie's. "All this talk is making me thirsty. Tea anyone?"

"Can a duck swim." Maddie could always drink tea.

"I have cupcakes ready to ice, if you're hungry?"

"You baked on your day off?"

"I love to bake, no matter the day. You know that."

It was true, and Maddie shouldn't be surprised since she was often guilty of doing exactly that. When you had nothing pressing, it proved to be the perfect time to try out a new recipe or two. They headed into the kitchen which looked out over the garden with the dining room opened up to see in both directions.

"Shall I frost the cupcakes? I could do with the practice." Laura asked.

"Yes, please," Gran answered as she made the tea in a pot showcasing the royal couple, Prince William and Kate.

Maddie collected three tea-sets from the shelves, each one a little different. Anyone lucky enough to be invited for tea on a regular basis was designated a particular set which included a side plate. This was a necessity since tea was always accompanied by something from Gran's repertoire of baking which changed with the seasons to coincide with what fruit was available and what she felt like baking.

Her set had a delicate pink rose depicted on two sides. Gran's had lilacs and now that Laura was living here, she had been given the blue wisteria pattern. When Suzy was around she had a set with orchids which were white with pink centers.

The sets were not randomly given. Gran insisted that each flower told something of the personality of the person using it. Loving to tease her Girlz, she never divulged what that might be and many hours had been spent trying to guess.

Maddie sat down at the table, feeling lazy and a little edgy that she wasn't out scouring the streets for Big Red, but it was nice to be with family and friends. No wonder Laura was coming along in leaps and bounds in her techniques at the bakery. With Gran as a private mentor she had already perfected a couple of recipes.

Cupcakes instead of breakfast was not the best as a rule, but on her day off the rules did not apply and therefore she had two. "Very nice, Gran, and superb frosting Laura. Is this a new recipe?"

"It is. Coffee and maple syrup."

"Mmmm. Delicious. The frosting too?"

Laura nodded shyly. "Cupcakes are a good seller at the bakery aren't they?"

"Everyone likes cupcakes." Maddie had to agree.

"You have a great selection of sweet things," she hesitated.

Maddie could see she had something on her mind. "Any ideas are welcome, we're a team after all."

Laura beamed. "There's been several queries about making bagels. Apparently they're a healthier option and you can add savory or sweet toppings."

"Bagels? I have made them of course, but I'm not sure how well they'll do in Maple Falls. When I initially chose which items to bake I didn't include them for that reason. People here like their fresh breads and buns. Still, they did do extremely well in Manhattan, and we're not as stretched for time now we have our new staff member." She winked at Laura. "And another about to start. If you like, we could give them a try."

"Wonderful, I can't wait. I love bagels, and Virginia

Bolton was asking about them too."

Maddie choked on a mouthful of tea at hearing the real estate broker was wanting to eat her food when she had denigrated the bakery not so long ago.

"I can't say that's an incentive to bake them."

Gran patted Maddie's hand as she passed her a napkin. "Now, now. She's paid her dues. Poor woman has been ostracized by the whole town for long enough, and her business is almost non-existent."

Maddie wiped her face on a napkin, her anger warring with compassion over the fear and drama Virginia had helped cause. "It's only been a few weeks. I can't say that I blame anyone for steering clear of her."

"Maddie, that's not how you were raised."

She dropped her head over the steaming cup at Gran's censure. "I know, but I'm still angry with her. We could have all been killed."

Virginia had helped the murderer up to a point, and insisted she didn't know how far Ralph Willis was prepared to go to get what he wanted.

"But we weren't. Remember, she had a mother she was protecting. Her reasons were valid to her."

"I know, but it's hard to let go of what might have happened if she hadn't come forward when she did."

"There you go. When it was needed she did the right thing. That's all anyone has to do in this life."

There was no way to fight that kind of optimism, so she changed the subject.

"Like I said, we can try making bagels and see how they go, but no promises to keep them on the schedule," she told both of them. Finishing her tea she stood. "I'm going to have another look around for Big Red. If either of you see him, could you give me a call?"

"We sure will. Have a lovely day and see you here for dinner?"

"Of course."

She left them with a heavy heart. It was sometimes hard living up to Gran's code of fairness, but there was no point trying to argue with it because once you gave it some thought she was usually right. Plus, her grandmother lived by that code every single day. Maddie shook her head with a small smile as she kept her eyes peeled for any sign of Big Red.

She called him several times, walking around the block and down to the green which was adjacent to the side of her shop, but he was nowhere to be found. It was still too early for most people to be out and about, and Maple Falls with its canopy of large Maple trees creating dappled light everywhere, was quiet and peaceful on a Saturday morning, unless there was a market happening.

The yoga group would be there soon and Maddie wondered for the umpteenth time if she should join them.

When she got back to her gate something shining in the grass caught her attention. Instantly she knew what it was. Bending she picked up Big Red's collar. Nobody would be calling her if someone found him because without this they wouldn't know where he belonged. Although, most of the town would have heard of Big Red, he was after all memorable.

Then she noticed that the collar was undone-not broken. What did that mean?

Ready to read more? Get your copy of Bagels and Blackmail today!

Recipes

These recipes are ones I use all the time and have come down the generations from my mum, grandmother, and some I have adapted from other recipes. Also, I now have my husband's grandmother's recipe book. Exciting! I'll be bringing some of them to life very soon.

Just a wee reminder, that I am a New Zealander. Occasionally I may have missed converting into ounces and pounds for my American readers.

My apologies for that, and please let me know—if you do try them—how they turn out.

Cheryl x

Easy Maple Syrup Cookie Recipe

Ingredients

1/2 lb / 250g butter (cut into small pieces, softened)
5oz / 140g caster sugar
10oz / 300g sifted all-purpose flour
1 egg yolk
4 tsp maple syrup

Instructions

1 Mix the butter and sugar together until it's light and fluffy-looking.
2 Break the egg and separate the yolk and white, keep the yolk and add it to the butter and sugar mix.
3 Mix in the maple syrup.
4 Add half the flour and mix well, then add the rest and mix slowly until you've got a nice dough that's not too wet.
5 Knead the dough into a ball. Leave it in the bowl and put it in the fridge for half an hour to chill.
6 Roll out the dough to about the thickness of your finger.
7 Cut circles with the rim of a clean glass, or use cookie cutters (gran uses maple leaf) to make shapes.

8 Grease a baking tray or use baking paper and lay out the cookies with a little gap between them.

9 Bake in a preheated oven at 180°C / 350°F (gas mark 4) for 12 to 15 minutes.

10 Don't forget that they will harden more when they've cooled so take them out of the oven when they are still a little bit soft.

11 Carefully slide them off the tray and cool on a rack.

12 Decorate them with frosting, and share with love!

Store in an air-tight container.

Gran's Apple Pie

Ingredients

8oz / 250g sifted all-purpose flour
5oz / 150g margarine or butter
4 tablespoons granulated sugar
1 large egg mixed with 3/4 of a cup of milk
5 cooking apples

Instructions

1 Preheat the oven to 200 C / Gas 6.
2 Peel and core the apples, then chop them up into fairly
large chunks. Put into a medium saucepan, add 4 tablespoons of granulated sugar and a half cup of water. 3 Cook
on medium to high heat, stirring constantly until the apples
are stewed. Set aside to cool a little.
4 Put flour, sugar and butter in a large bowl. Rub the mix
until it looks like breadcrumbs. Make a hole in the mix, then
add the egg and milk.
5 Cut the mix with a knife until it forms a dough. Add a
little more milk if you need to.
6 Knead the dough for a couple of minutes. Cut it in half,

leaving one half to the side. Knead the first half a little more, then roll out with a rolling pin. Dust a pie plate with some flour, then place your rolled-out dough on the plate and trim the edge.

7 Roll out the second ball of dough and leave to one side.

8 Place the stewed apples in your prepared pie dish, then put your rolled-out second half of dough on top and trim around the edge to take the excess dough away.

9 Make several cuts on the top of the pie. Seal the edges with a fork. This is less sticky if you dip your fork in some flour in between.

10 If you have leftover pastry, you can make shapes to decorate. (Gran likes her maple leaf, but you can use any shape you like.)

11 Place pie on the middle shelf in the oven. Baking takes around 20-25 minutes. The pie should be golden brown.

12 Remove and eat hot or leave to cool. Either way, you can add a dollop of cream or ice cream. Gran likes to sprinkle confectioner's sugar (icing sugar) over the top like snow.

Tip: Roll the dough over your rolling pin to help place it on the pie dish, which will help you avoid cracking or tears.

Also by C. A. Phipps

The Maple Lane Cozy Mysteries

Sugar and Sliced - Maple Lane Prequel

Apple Pie and Arsenic

Bagels and Blackmail

Cookies and Chaos

Doughnuts and Disaster

Eclairs and Extortion

Fudge and Frenemies

Gingerbread and Gunshots

Honey Cake and Homicide - preorder now!

Midlife Potions - Paranormal Cozy Mysteries

Witchy Awakening

Witchy Hot Spells

Witchy Flash Back

Witchy Bad Blood - preorder now!

Beagle Diner Cozy Mysteries

Beagles Love Cupcake Crimes

Beagles Love Steak Secrets

Beagles Love Muffin But Murder

Beagles Love Layer Cake Lies

The Cozy Café Mysteries

Sweet Saboteur

Candy Corruption

Mocha Mayhem

Berry Betrayal

Deadly Desserts

Please note: Most are also available in paperback and some in audio.

Remember to join Cheryl's Cozy Mystery newsletter.

There's a free recipe book waiting for you. ;-)

Cheryl also writes romance as Cheryl Phipps.

About the Author

'Life is a mystery. Let's follow the clues together.'

C. A. Phipps is a USA Today best-selling author from beautiful New Zealand. Cheryl is an empty-nester living in a quiet suburb with her wonderful husband, 'himself'. With an extended family to keep her busy when she's not writing, there is just enough space for a crazy mixed breed dog who stole her heart! She enjoys family times, baking, and her quest for the perfect latte.

Check out her website http://caphipps.com

facebook.com/authorcaphipps

x.com/CherylAPhipps

instagram.com/caphippsauthor

Made in the USA
Middletown, DE
18 August 2024

59390259R00170